THE BASKET WOMAN

WESTERN LITERATURE SERIES

The BASKET WOMAN

A Book of Indian Tales

MARY AUSTIN

Foreword by Mark Schlenz

University of Nevada Press

Reno   Las Vegas

WESTERN LITERATURE SERIES

University of Nevada Press, Reno, Nevada 89557 USA
www.unpress.nevada.edu
Copyright © 1904 by Mary Austin as *The Basket Woman:*
A Book of Fanciful Tales for Children
New material copyright © 1999 by University of Nevada Press
Manufactured in the United States of America
Design by Erin Kirk New

Library of Congress Cataloging-in-Publication Data
Austin, Mary Hunter, 1868–1934
The basket woman : a book of Indian tales / Mary Austin ;
foreword by Mark Schlenz.
p.   cm. — (Western literature series)
ISBN 978-0-87417-336-9 (pbk. : alk. paper)
1. Indians of North America — California — Owens River
Valley — Social life and customs — Fiction. 2. Paiute Indians —
Social life and customs — Fiction. I. Title. II. Series.
PS3501.U8B37   1999
813'.52 — dc21   98-27733
CIP

The paper used in this book meets the requirements of American
National Standard for Information Sciences — Permanence of Paper
for Printed Library materials, ANSI Z39.48-1984. Binding
materials were selected for strength and durability.

This book has been reproduced as a digital reprint.

CONTENTS

Foreword by Mark Schlenz vii

Preface xvii

The Basket Woman—First Story 1

The Basket Woman—Second Story 9

The Stream That Ran Away 16

The Coyote-Spirit and the Weaving Woman 22

The Cheerful Glacier 30

The Merry-Go-Round 36

The Christmas Tree 44

The Fire Bringer 54

The Crooked Fir 60

The Sugar Pine 65

The Golden Fortune 71

The White-Barked Pine 82

Na'Ÿang-Wit'e, The First Rabbit Drive 87

Mahala Joe 93

v

FOREWORD

The sketches and tales first published together in 1904 under the title *The Basket Woman* were born out of Mary Hunter Austin's struggle against frontier and personal hardships for economic survival and artistic expression in the desert regions of the eastern Sierra. In 1888 Austin's arrival at age eighteen with her fatherless family at a futile homestead in an unirrigated and remote portion of California's lower San Joaquin Valley adjacent to the Tejon Ranch coincided with one of the more catastrophic droughts in the history of western settlement. It was during this drought, under the tutelage of the Tejon's colorful owner, General Beale, that Mary first began to perceive fundamental dynamics of environmental and cultural patterns in ecological contexts. General Beale, a former California Indian commissioner, had removed scattered remnants of several local tribes into rancherias on his vast holdings. From her observations of Native Americans during the extended drought, Austin later wrote in *Earth Horizon*, her third-person autobiography, that,

> she began to learn how Indians live off a land upon which more sophisticated races would starve, and how the land itself instructed them. As she saw these things, the whole basis of her social philosophy and economy altered beyond the capacity of books to keep pace with it. She was altered herself to an extent

and in a direction that nothing she has yet written fully expresses.
(198)

By the fall of 1889 the continued failure of the Hunter family
homestead in California's climate of drought and increasingly
hostile local water rights struggles forced Mary into her tenta-
tive career as a visiting schoolteacher among children of the
employees of Mountain View Dairy, "one of a chain of similarly
owned company ranches in the very heart of the disputed sec-
tion, in which long-settled general farmers made cause with the
newcomers for water privileges" (*Earth Horizon* 207). During
her travels among the farmers, Austin "gathered that intensely
particularized knowledge of the Western scene which is gar-
nered in her books" (*Earth Horizon* 208).

In 1891 Mary's family abandoned the failed homestead venture for a small ranch outside of Bakersfield, California, and
Mary, by marrying Wallace Austin, embarked upon yet another
stage of her struggle to make the West her home—this time not
as the sister of a failed farmer, but as the wife of a failed water
developer. In 1892 Wallace Austin brought his pregnant bride to
Inyo County, into the region of the Owens Valley and surround-
ing desert basins and ranges east of the Sierra Nevada—"into
that region which is still largely known by the name she gave it,
'The Land of Little Rain'" (*Earth Horizon* 232). When the Aus-
tins' ditch company failed several weeks later, Mary was rudely
evicted from their lodgings at the Lone Pine Hotel and began the
long struggle to pull her small family through the bankruptcy.
The first of her stories, woven from strands of tales she had
gathered on the Tejon and Mountain View Dairy Ranches, was
published in the *Overland* while she was abed with the birth of

her daughter. Through the following ten years of her marriage, while Wallace's career continued to founder, Mary contributed her earnings from school teaching and the publication of her short stories toward financing her family out of the debts incurred by her husband's irrigation ventures.

Her first collection of sketches and tales, *The Land of Little Rain*, published in 1903, began to bring Austin the financial reward and literary recognition for which she had labored during this desperate period—and it remains the work for which she is best known even today. One of the most memorable sketches of that work, the poignant portrait of *Seyavi* the "Basket Maker," apparently haunted Austin so strongly that in the year following her initial success she refashioned her basket-maker figure into a central protagonist, sometime narrative voice, and title character of her second collection of tales. Many of the stories collected in *The Basket Woman*, written during the same period of struggle as the material that became *The Land of Little Rain*, had already been published singly in major publications such as the *Atlantic Monthly, Cosmopolitan*, and *Saint Nicholas*. They can be read here still, of course, as individual narrative pieces of considerable charm and merit, but in *The Basket Woman*, even more significantly than in *The Land of Little Rain*, Austin's strategic organizational arrangement of tales creates a powerful framing narrative in which the effect of the whole far transcends the sum of the individual pieces.

In "The Basket Woman" sketch from *The Land of Little Rain*, Austin wrote that, "To understand the fashion of any life, one must know the land it is lived in and the procession of the year." The tales of *The Basket Woman* share the intense focus of the naturalist's perspective developed in her earlier work, but as she structured their arrangement in her second collection, Austin also lifted her appreciative gaze from a study of uniquely adapted flora, fauna, and human life in the arid lands she shared on the late frontier to examine the dramatic implications of a legacy of conquest upon the land and its native peoples. In *The Basket Woman*, more directly than in much of her better-known work, Austin boldly confronts brutal environmental realities and cultural conflicts of American expansionism in the West.

To read *The Basket Woman* as an ecological and multicultural examination of American expansionism requires deeper literary appreciation of Austin's subtle organizational arrangement strategies. On the surface, *The Basket Woman* presents itself as a volume of western children's stories. Austin claimed her teaching experience in the West had shown her that stories she composed and set in the landscapes of the region in which her students lived had more relevance to their developing understanding of environmental conditions of life and the subtleties of human relations than classical myths or the American literature of New England. Certainly the individual tales of *The Basket Woman* will amply reward a reading at the elementary level of children's literature and, at the same time, provide worthwhile environmental education in the natural history of the region. However, deeper and more sophisticated appreciation of Austin's larger ecological and social purpose and accomplishment requires reading across the gaps between stories—a reading in which the reader is enlisted to develop a connective thematic comprehension from the accumulated inferences in the sequence of tales.

This type of literary effect, generated by what has been termed a "divided narrative," characterizes much of the greatest of

American literature concerned with effects of conquest upon the American continent and its peoples. Contemporary Native American writers such as N. Scott Momaday, Louise Erdrich, and Leslie Marmon Silko are perhaps directly indebted to William Faulkner in their deployment of the technique of divided narrative. Both Faulkner and Ernest Hemingway in the Nick Adams stories are traditionally regarded as having literary antecedent for their narrative methods in Sherwood Anderson's *Winesburg Ohio* of 1919. More recently, however, commentators on American literary history have begun to recognize women's regional fiction of the turn of the twentieth century as the literary origin of the divided narrative. With some obvious acknowledgment of her predecessor Sarah Orne Jewett and *The Country of Pointed Firs*, Austin's *The Land of Little Rain* may well deserve recognition as one of the first instances of what has become a widely practiced and celebrated American narrative form. Certainly, thematic development generated by the particular sequence of stories in *The Basket Woman* reflects the conscious intentions of a literary imagination not bound by limits of any single tale.

The first two stories of *The Basket Woman* introduce the collection's frame narrative and establish the methodical pattern of juxtaposition and contrast that generates Austin's more subtle thematic development throughout the work. In these two stories, Austin initiates her readers and the character of a newly arrived homesteader's son named Alan to a historic appreciation of Native American culture and to the plight of postconquest Indian peoples. In the first of these stories, Austin contrasts impressions of indolence and squalor from Alan's initial visit to an Indian campoodie with visions of native industry and well-being glimpsed in his dream journey with the Basket Woman to the old times, when sustaining interrelations of native peoples and a nurturing environment had not yet been displaced by incoming homesteaders. In the Basket Woman's second story, Austin then inverts Alan's commentary on the contrast of pre- and postconquest native life developed in the first story when in a second dream journey the Basket Woman exposes Alan to disturbing visions of intertribal warfare and ensuing famine. At the conclusion of the second story, Alan draws a simplistic conclusion from the contrasts witnessed, saying, "Do you know, I think Indians are a great deal better off as they are now." While a naive reader of the tales might accept this conclusion as adequate, Austin's juxtapositions develop enough substantial irony and ambiguity to demand far more reflection upon historical progress than a child's pat and sentimental resolution of an ongoing cultural conflict.

Austin proceeds to deepen the irony and ambiguity undercutting Alan's simplistic sentiment—and further sophisticates her treatment of the environmental and cultural histories of the region—through her strategic organizational arrangement of the collection's subsequent tales. In the intervening tales leading to the book's conclusion, the Basket Woman sometimes steps back as a character to assume the role of narrator through which Austin retells stories she had gathered in her visits to neighboring Indian villages. In other tales, Austin herself adopts a more native sensibility toward the natural world as she personifies streams and trees and birds and glaciers to convey a living sense of the natural history of her region. Midway through the sequence of stories, in "The Merry-Go-Round," the Basket Woman character reemerges as a central protagonist.

In the opening stories, Austin develops a surrogate maternal relation between Alan and the Basket Woman in which her great cone-shaped basket becomes a sort of symbolic womb from which Alan's consciousness, emerging from the world of mythic dream Indians into actual association with local Paiutes, is born again into new perceptions of nature and native life. In "The Merry-Go-Round," Austin strengthens this maternal relation as the Basket Woman physically rescues Alan from near death in the desert and thus delivers him once more into a deepened understanding of life in the land. As the Basket Woman educates Alan by involving him in her domestic tasks and telling tales that emphasize the connectedness and interdependence of communal life lived in cooperation with the natural world, she offers him a more feminine alternative to patriarchal myths and ideologies of conquest and manifest destiny. It is within this context that the final story of *The Basket Woman,* an unforgettable tale of honor and endurance titled "Mahala Joe," acquires a peculiar strength of irony.

The collection's final story makes Austin's valorization of a feminized sensibility as personified in the character of the Basket Woman even more graphically and ironically manifest through the transformation of a would-be warrior into a *mahala,* Austin's local term for an Indian woman. Though Mahala Joe wears a woman's skirt as tribal punishment for cowardice in battle, readers learn that this "badge of an all but intolerable shame" actually signifies his transcendent honor, his courageous loyalty to a white brother. The significant historic relocation of this story to the Paiute wars of the mid-nineteenth century displaces Alan with an earlier homesteader's son named Walter who, as a result of his own mother's death in childbirth, is given over to a nursing Indian woman for rearing. Walter and the Indian woman's son, whom Walter names Joe after his own father, grow together as inseparable friends and eventually take a ritual blood-brother oath. When hostility later breaks out between the settlers and the tribes, the boys promise not to attack each others' homes. Walter, however, enjoys considerable privilege in this arrangement and, unbeknownst to Joe, Walter's father quickly sends him back east for schooling to avoid the troubles. Walter never returns. On the other hand, Joe, because he keeps faith and refuses to join in the attack on the house of Walter's father, bears his lifelong ignominy among the defeated remains of his people in stoic silence.

Austin's substitution of "Mahala Joe" for a story that would resolve narrative dynamics she generates between Alan and the Basket Woman establishes ambivalences and ambiguities that undermine sentimental interpretations of the preceding stories and suspend resolution of the collection's framing narrative. Later in her career, Austin prophesied that the American Southwest would become the hearth of the next great world culture through an environmentally informed synthesis of the indigenous primitive and newly arrived modern cultural values that met there. Throughout the text of *The Basket Woman*, Austin struggles with Alan's, and her reader's, evolving consciousness to give birth to an Americanized white man, a white man who evolves by virtue of a feminized sensitivity to the subtleties of the teachings of the American earth and to the necessity of multicultural social cooperation to perceive and pursue a reformed, sustainable vision of human destiny. But the failure of Austin's optimistic prophecy so painfully evident from our current historical perspective is ironically presaged by the narrative vanishings of her white Indians—Alan's *and* Walter's—and by the weight of injustice blighting her own story of Mahala Joe.

Through the progress of *The Basket Woman* stories, Euro-American characters and readers gain glimpses of the cultural and environmental wisdom of a region's indigenous inhabitants, but any reformation of their own dominant culture remains, as evidenced by Alan's unexplained disappearance from the narrative, finally incomplete. Austin's final, problematic representation of a Native American man and his postconquest culture further underscores the absence of her fully Americanized white man. Mahala Joe's presence, which ironically registers the cross-fertilization of cultural contact upon his people, obstructs the progress of the classic frontier myth fueled by the stereotypical "vanishing American" disappearance of the Indian.

What begins in *The Basket Woman* tales as a process of feminizing and Americanizing the perspectives and characters of white men concludes not with the presence of socially and environmentally reformed Euro-Americans, but ends instead with the ironic valorization of a red man in skirts who perseveres in their absence. Mahala Joe cannot be seen, however, as the classic "vanishing American" in this text any more than he or the Basket Woman herself can be seen stereotypically as a new generation of Pocahontas's daughters conveniently facilitating the course of conquest. Mahala Joe is a survivor, a master of adaptation forever faithful to his communal bonds and always responsive to the evolving exigencies of his social and physical environments. He is a challenging figure for the received stereotypes of Native Americans current in the cultural imagination of Austin's period, a figure demanding the appreciation of enlightened social observers. Austin's treatment of this native character is progressive to the extent that she presents Mahala Joe as a portrait of endurance. Still, her picture is incomplete in that her tales do not depict white characters fully capable of the appreciation this survivor of conquest merits. This task of appreciation is reserved instead for Austin's readers. It is the challenge Austin faced from the delimiting cultural circumstances of her time in attempting throughout her life to identify and rectify the crucial injustices of Indian-white relations; it is the challenge that confronts us still.

MARK SCHLENZ

PREFACE

All of these stories are so nearly true that you need not be troubled in the least about believing them. They all occurred in that strip of country which lies east of the Sierra Nevada mountains and south of Yosemite. All the names of places are as you will find them on the map, except the Indian names. Indian names for places all mean something in particular, as *Pahrump,* which is a Paiute word, signifying that this is a place where there is water enough to raise corn, and might be applied to any place answering that description.

The customs and manners are all as they may be found in the many small clans of the Paiutes; but it really ought to be spelled Pah Utes, for it means The Utes Who Live by the Water, to distinguish them from the Utes who live in the Great Basin, where there are almost no running streams. These clans are so mixed together now by marriage and by the breaking down of old tribal usages that it is not possible to say in which clan the tales originated, and they have become changed and confused, very much as we know the old tales of Greeks and Romans to be. The words "mahala" and "campoodie" are not Indian words, but they are used by Indians as well as by white men all over the Pacific Coast, the first to designate an Indian woman, and the second a village or collection of huts. No one knows quite how "mahala" came to be used. It might be a word belonging to some tribe that white men first became acquainted with, and it has been surmised to be a mispronunciation of the Spanish *mujer,* meaning woman. "Campoodie" is from the Spanish *campo,* and is often pronounced and spelled "campody." A wickiup, as every one in the West knows, is a hut of reeds or brush, very often pieced out with blankets and tin cans.

I know that the story of the Coyote-Spirit is true, because the Basket Woman told it to me, and evidently believed it. She said she had seen Coyote-Spirits herself in Saline Valley and at Fish Lake. In the same way she told me about The Fire Bringer, and Kern River Jim told me of Tavwots and how it happens that there are no trees on the high mountains. And if this last is not true, how are you going to account for the fact that there really are no trees there? As for Mahala Joe, he lives and wears his woman's dress at Big Pine, and if this account of how he came by it is not just as it happened, it might very well be; for he is not the first Indian who has adopted woman's dress to escape going to war, though there are no others left in this district.

I know that the story of the Crooked Fir is true, because if you come up the Kearsarge trail with me I can show you the very tree, and also the place where the White Bark Pine stood; for I was one of the party that took it on its travels over the mountain: and the rest of the stories are all as true as these.

THE BASKET WOMAN

THE BASKET WOMAN

First Story

The homesteader's cabin stood in a moon-shaped hollow between the hills and the high mesa; and the land before it stretched away golden and dusky green, and was lost in a blue haze about where the river settlements began. The hills had a flowing outline and melted softly into each other and higher hills behind, until the range broke in a ragged crest of thin peaks white with snow. A clean, wide sky bent over that country, and the air that moved in it was warm and sweet.

The homesteader's son had run out on the trail that led toward the spring, with half a mind to go to it, but ran back again when he saw the Basket Woman coming. He was afraid of her, and ashamed because he was afraid, so he did not tell his mother that he had changed his mind.

"There is the mahala coming for the wash," said his mother; "now you will have company at the spring." But Alan only held tighter to a fold of her dress. This was the third time the Indian woman had come to wash for the homesteader's wife; and, though she was slow and quiet and had a pleasant smile, Alan was still afraid of her. All that he had heard of Indians before coming to this country was very frightful, and he did not understand yet that it was not so. Beyond a certain point of hills on clear days he could see smoke rising from the campoodie, and

1

though he knew nothing but his dreams of what went on there, he would not so much as play in that direction.

The Basket Woman was the only Indian that he had seen. She would come walking across the mesa with a great cone-shaped carrier basket heaped with brushwood on her shoulders, stooping under it and easing the weight by a buckskin band about her forehead. Sometimes it would be a smaller basket carried in the same fashion, and she would be filling it with bulbs of wild hyacinth or taboose; often she carried a bottle-necked water basket to and from the spring, and always wore a bowl-shaped basket on her head for a hat. Her long hair hung down from under it, and her black eyes glittered beadily below the rim. Alan had a fancy that any moment she might pick him up with a quick toss as if be had been a bit of brushwood, and drop him over her shoulder into the great carrier, and walk away across the mesa with him. So when he saw her that morning coming down the trail from the spring, he hung close by his mother's skirts.

"You must not be afraid of her, Alan," said his mother; "she is very kind, and no doubt has had a boy of her own."

The Basket Woman showed them her white, even teeth in a smile. "This one very pretty boy," she said; but Alan had made up his mind not to trust her. He was thinking of what the teamster had said when he had driven them up from the railroad station with their belongings the day they came to their new home and found the Basket Woman spying curiously in at the cabin windows.

"You wanter watch out how you behaves yourself, sonny," said the teamster, wagging a solemn jaw, "she's likely to pack you away in that basket o' her'n one of these days." And Alan had watched out very carefully indeed.

It was not a great while after they came to the foothill claim that the homesteader went over to the campoodie to get an Indian to help at fence building, and Alan went with him, holding fast by his father's hand. They found the Indians living in low, foul huts; their clothes were also dirty, and they sat about on the ground, fat and good-natured. The dogs and children lay sleeping in the sun. It was all very disappointing.

"Will they not hurt us, father?" Alan had said at starting.

"Oh, no, my boy; you must not get any such notion as that," said the homesteader; "Indians are not at all now what they were once."

Alan thought of this as he looked at the campoodie, and pulled at his father's hand.

"I do not like Indians the way they are now," he said; and immediately saw that he had made a mistake, for he was standing directly in front of the Basket Woman's hut, and as she suddenly put her head out of the door he thought by the look of her mysterious, bright eyes that she had understood. He did not venture to say anything more, and all the way home kept looking back toward the campoodie to see if anything came of it.

"Why do you not eat your supper?" said his mother. "I am afraid the long walk in the hot sun was too much for you." Alan dared not say anything to her of what troubled him, though perhaps it would have been better if he had, for that night the Basket Woman came for him.

She did not pick him up and toss him over her shoulder as he expected; but let down the basket, and he stepped into it of his own accord. Alan was surprised to find that he was not so much afraid of her after all.

"What will you do with me?" he said.

"I will show you Indians as they used to be," said she.

Alan could feel the play of her strong shoulders as they went out across the lower mesa and began to climb the hills.

"Where do you go?" said the boy.

"To Pahrump, the valley of Corn Water. It was there my people were happiest in old days."

They went on between the oaks, and smelled the musky sweet smell of the wild grapevines along the water borders. The sagebrush began to fail from the slopes, and buckthorn to grow up tall and thicker; the wind brought them a long sigh from the lowest pines. They came up with the silver firs and passed them, passed the drooping spruces, the wet meadows, and the wood of thimble-cone pines. The air under them had an earthy smell. Presently they came out upon a cleared space very high up where the rocks were sharp and steep.

"Why are there no trees here?" asked Alan.

"I will tell you about that," said the Basket Woman. "In the old flood time, and that is longer ago than is worth counting, the water came up and covered the land, all but the high tops of mountains. Here then the Indians fled and lived, and with them the animals that escaped from the flood. There were trees growing then over all the high places, but because the waters were long on the earth the Indians were obliged to cut them down for firewood. Also they killed all the large animals for food, but the small ones hid in the rocks. After that the waters went down; trees and grass began to grow over all the earth, but never any more on the tops of high mountains. They had all been burned off. You can see that it is so."

From the top of the mountain Alan could see all the hills on the other side shouldering and peering down toward the happy valley of Corn Water.

"Here," said the Basket Woman, "my people came of old time in the growing season of the year; they planted corn, and the streams came down from the hills and watered it. Now we, too, will go down."

They went by a winding trail, steep and stony. The pines stood up around and locked them closely in.

"I see smoke arising," said Alan, "blue smoke above the pines."

"It is the smoke of their hearth fires," said the Basket Woman, and they went down and down.

"I hear a sound of singing," said the boy.

"It is the women singing and grinding at the quern," she said, and her feet went faster.

"I hear laughter," he said again, "it mixes with the running of the water."

"It is the maidens washing their knee-long hair. They kneel by the water and stoop down, they dip in the running water and shake out bright drops in the sun."

"There is a pleasant smell," said Alan.

"It is pine nuts roasting in the cones," said the Basket Woman; "so it was of old time."

They came out of the cleft of the hills in a pleasant place by singing water. "There you will see the rows of wickiups," said the Basket Woman, "with the doors all opening eastward to the sun. Let us sit here and see what we shall see."

The women sat by the wickiups weaving baskets of willow and stems of fern. They made patterns of bright feathers and strung wampum about the rims. Some sewed with sinew and needles of cactus thorn on deerskin white and fine; others winnowed the corn. They stood up tossing it in baskets like grains of gold, and the wind carried away the chaff. All this time the young girls were laughing as they dried their hair in the sun. They bound it with flowers and gay strings of beads, and made their cheeks bright with red earth. The children romped and shouted about the camp, and ran bare-legged in the stream.

"Do they do nothing but play?" said Alan.

"You shall see," said the Basket Woman.

Away up the mountain sounded a faint halloo. In a moment all the camp was bustle and delight. The children clapped their hands; they left off playing and began to drag up brushwood for the fires. The women put away their weaving and brought out the cooking pots; they heard the men returning from the hunt. The young men brought deer upon their shoulders; one had grouse and one held up a great basket of trout. The women made the meat ready for cooking. Some of them took meal and made cakes for baking in the ashes. The men rested in the glow of the fires, feathering arrows and restringing their bows.

"That is well," said the Basket Woman, "to make ready for tomorrow's meat before to-day's is eaten."

"How happy they are!" said the boy.

"They will be happier when they have eaten," said she.

After supper the Indians gathered together for singing and dancing. The old men told tales one after the other, and the children thought each one was the best. Between the tales the Indians all sang together, or one sang a new song that he had made. There was one of them who did better than all. He had streaked his body with colored earth and had a band of eagle

feathers in his hair. In his hand was a rattle of wild sheep's horn
and small stones; he kept time with it as he leapt and sang in the
light of the fire. He sang of old wars, sang of the deer that was
killed, sang of the dove and the young grass that grew on the
mountain; and the people were well pleased, for when the heart
is in the singing it does not matter much what the song is about.
The men beat their hands together to keep time to his dancing,
and the earth under his feet was stamped to a fine dust.

"He is one that has found the wolf's song," said the Basket Woman.

"What is that?" asked Alan.

"It is an old tale of my people," said she. "Once there was a
man who could not make any songs, so he got no praise from
the tribe, and it troubled him much. Then, as he was gathering
taboose by the river, a wolf went by, and the wolf said to him,
'What will you have me to give you for your taboose?' Then said
the man, 'I will have you to give me a song.'

"'That will I gladly,' said the wolf. So the wolf taught him,
and that night he sang the wolf's song in the presence of all the
people, and it made their hearts to burn within them. Then the
man fell down as if he were dead, for the pure joy of singing,
and when deep sleep was upon him the wolf came in the night
and stole his song away. Neither the man nor any one who had
heard it remembered it any more. So we say when a man sings
as no other sang before him, 'He has the wolf's song.' It is a good
saying. Now we must go, for the children are all asleep by their
mothers, and the day comes soon," said the Basket Woman.
"Shall we come again?" said Alan. "And will it all be as it is now?"

"My people come often to the valley of Corn Water," said she, "but it is never as it is now except in dreams. Now we must go quickly." Far up the trail they saw a grayness in the eastern sky where the day was about to come in.

"Hark," said the Basket Woman, "they sing together the coyote song. It is so that they sing it when the coyote goes home from his hunting, and the morning is near.

"The coyote cries . . .
He cries at daybreak . . .
He cries . . .
The coyote cries" . . .

sang the Basket Woman, but all the spaces in between the words were filled with long howls,—weird, wicked noises that seemed to hunt and double in a half-human throat. It made the hair on Alan's neck stand up, and cold shivers creep along his back. He began to shake, for the wild howls drew near and louder, and he felt the bed under him tremble with his trembling.

"Mother, mother," he cried, "what is that?"

"It is only the coyotes," said she; "they always howl about this time of night. It is nothing; go to sleep again."

"But I am afraid."

"They cannot hurt you," said his mother; "it is only the little gray beasts that you see trotting about the mesa of afternoons; hear them now."

"I am afraid," said Alan.

"Then you must come in my bed," said she; and in a few minutes he was fast asleep again.

THE BASKET WOMAN

Second Story

ᶦᵐⁱᵐⁱᵐⁱᵐⁱᵐ

The next time Alan saw the Basket Woman he was not nearly so
much afraid of her, though he did not venture to speak of their
journey to Pahrump. He said to his mother, "Do you wish the
Indians could have stayed the way they were?" and his mother
laughed.

"Why, no, child," she said, "I do not think that I do. I think
they are much better off as they are now." Alan, however, was
not to be convinced. The next time he saw the Basket Woman
he was even troubled about it.

The homesteader had taken his family to the town for a day,
and the first thing Alan saw when he got down from the wagon
was the Basket Woman. She was sitting in a corner of the side-
walk with a group of other mahalas, with her blanket drawn
over her shoulders, looking out upon the town, and her eyes
were dull and strange.

A stream of people went by them in the street, and minded
them no more than the dogs they stepped over, sprawling at
the doors of the stores. Some of the Indian women had children
with them, but they neither shouted nor ran as they had done
in the camp of Corn Water; they sat quietly by their mothers,
and Alan noticed how worn and poor were the clothes of all of
them, and how wishful all the eyes. He could not get his mind
off them because he could not get them out of his sight for very

long at a time. It was a very small town, and as he went with his mother in and about the stores he would be coming face to face with mahalas every little while, and the Basket Woman's eyes were always sad.

His mother, when she had finished her shopping, gave him a silver dime and told him that he might spend it as he wished. As soon as Alan had turned the corner on that errand there was the Basket Woman with her chin upon her knees and her blanket drawn over her shoulders. Alan stopped a moment in front of her; he would have liked to say something comforting, but found himself still afraid.

Her eyes looked on beyond him, blurred and dim; he supposed she must be thinking of the happy valley, and grew so very sorry for her that, as he could not get the courage to speak, he threw his dime into her lap and ran as fast as he could away. It seemed to him as he ran that she called to him, but he could not be sure.

That night, almost as soon as he had touched the pillow, she came and stood beside him without motion or sound, and let down the basket from her back.

"Do we go to Corn Water?" asked Alan as he stepped into it.

"To my people of old time," said the Basket Woman, "so that you need not be so much sorry."

Then they went out by the mesa trail, where the sage showed duskily under a thin rim of moon. It seemed to Alan that they went slowly, almost heavily. When they came to the parting of the ways, she let down the basket to rest. A rabbit popped, startled, out of the brush, and scurried into the dark; its white tail, like a signal, showed the way it went.

"What was that?" asked Alan.

"Only little Tavwots, whom we scared out of his nest. Lean forward," she said, "and I will tell you a tale about him." So the boy leaned his head against the Basket Woman's long black hair, and heard the story of Little Tavwots and How He Caught the Sun in a Snare.

"It was long ago," said the Basket Woman. "Tavwots was the largest of all four-footed things, and a mighty hunter. He would get up as soon as it was day and go to his hunting, but always before him was the track of a great foot on the trail; and this troubled him, for his pride was as big as his body and greater than his fame.

"'Who is this?' cried Tavwots, 'that goes with so great a stride before me to the hunting? Does he think to put me to shame?'

"'T'-sst!' said his mother, 'there is none greater than thee.'

"'Nevertheless,' said Tavwots, 'there are the footprints in the trail.' The next morning he got up earlier, but there was always the great footprints and the long stride before him.

"'Now I will set me a trap for this impudent fellow,' said Tavwots, for he was very cunning. So he made a snare of his bowstring and set it in the trail overnight, and in the morning when he went to look, behold, he had caught the sun in his snare. All that quarter of the earth was beginning to smoke with the heat of it.

"'Is it you?' cried Tavwots, 'who made the tracks in my trail?'

"'It is I,' said the sun. 'Come now and set me free before the whole earth is afire.' Then Tavwots saw what he had to do, so he drew his knife and ran to cut the bowstring. But the heat was so great that he ran back before he had done it, and was melted down to one half his size. Then the smoke of the burning earth began to curl up against the sky.

11

"'Come again, Tavwots,' cried the sun. So he ran again and ran back, and the third time he ran he cut the bowstring, and the sun was set free from the snare. But by that time Tavwots was melted down to as small as he is now, and so he remains. Still you may see by the print of his feet as he leaps in the trail how great his stride was when he caught the sun in his snare.

"So it is always," said the Basket Woman, "that which is large grows less, and my people, which were great, have dwindled away."

After that she became quiet, and they went on over the mountain. Because he was beginning to be acquainted with it, the way seemed shorter to Alan than before. They passed over the high barren ridges, and he began to look for the camp at Corn Water.

"I see no smoke," said Alan.

"It would bring down their enemies like buzzards on carrion," said the Basket Woman.

"There is no sound of singing nor of laughter," said the boy.

"Who laughs in the time of war?" said she.

"Is there war?" asked Alan.

"Long and bitter," said the Basket Woman. "Let us go softly and come upon them unawares."

So they went, light of foot, among the pines until they saw the wickiups opening eastward to the sun, but many of them stood ruined and awry. There were only the very old and the children in the camp, and these did not run and play. They stole about like mice in the meadow sod, and if so much as a twig snapped in the forest, they huddled motionless as young quail. The women worked in the growing corn; they dug roots on the hill slope and caught the grasshoppers for food. One made a noose of her long black hair plucked out, and snared the bright

12

lizards that ran among the rocks. It seemed to Alan that the Indians looked wishful and thinner than they should; but such food as they found was all put by.

"Why do they do this?" asked the boy.

"That the men who go to war may not go fasting," said the Basket Woman. "Look, now we shall have news of them."

A young man came noiselessly out of the wood, and it was he who had sung the new song on the night of feasting and dancing. He had eagle feathers in his hair, but they were draggled; there was beadwork on his leggings, but it was torn with thorns; there was paint on his face and his body, but it was smeared over red, and as he came into the camp he broke his bow across his knee.

"It is a token of defeat," said the Basket Woman; "the others will come soon." But some came feebly because of wounds, and it seemed the women looked for some who might never come. They cast up their arms and cried with a terrible wailing sound that rose and shuddered among the pines.

"Be still," said the young man; "would you bring our enemies down upon us with your screeching?" Then the women threw themselves quietly in the dust, and rocked to and fro with sobbing; their stillness was more bitter than their crying.

Suddenly out of the wood came a storm of arrows, a rush of strange, painted braves, and the din of fighting.

"Shut your eyes," said the Basket Woman, "it is not good for you to see." Alan hid his face in the Basket Woman's dress, and heard the noise of fighting rage and die away. When he ventured to look again on the ruined huts and the trampled harvest, there were few left in the camp of Corn Water, and they had enough to do to find food for their poor bodies. They winnowed the creek with basket-work weirs for every finger-long troutling that came down in it, and tore the bark off the pine trees to get at the grubs underneath.

"Why do they not go out and kill deer as before?" asked Alan.

"Their enemies lurk in the wood and drive away the game," said the Basket Woman.

"Why do they not go to another place?"

"Where shall they go, when their foes watch every pass?" said she.

It seemed to Alan that many days and nights passed while they watched by the camp; and the days were all sorrowful, and always, as before, the best meat was set aside for the strongest.

"Why is this so?" asked the boy.

"Because," said the Basket Woman, "those who are strong must stay so to care for the rest. It is the way of my people. You see that the others do not complain." And it was so that the feeble ones tottered silently about the camp or sat still a long time in one place with their heads upon their knees.

"How will it end?" asked Alan.

"They must go away at last," said she, "though the cords of their hearts are fastened here. But there is no seed corn, and the winter is close at hand."

Then there began to be a tang of frost in the air, and the people gathered up their household goods, and, though there was not much of them, they staggered and bent under the burden as they went up out of the once happy valley to another home. The women let down their long hair and smeared ashes upon it; they threw up their lean arms and wailed long and mournfully as they passed among the pines. Alan began to tremble with crying, and felt the Basket Woman patting him on the shoulder. Her voice sounded to him like the voice of his mother telling him to go to sleep again, for there was nothing for him to be troubled about. After he grew quieter, the Indian woman lifted him up. "We must be going," she said, "it is not good for us to be here."

Alan wished as they went up over the mountain that she would help him with talk toward forgetting what he had seen, but the long hair fell over her face and she would not talk. He shivered in the basket, and the night felt colder and full of fearsome noises.

"What is that?" he whispered, as a falling star trailed all across the dark.

"It is the coyote people that brought the fire to my people," said the Basket Woman. Alan hoped she would tell him a tale about it, but she would not. They went on down the mountain until they came to the borders of the long-leaved pines. Alan heard the sough of the wind in the needles, and it seemed as if it called.

"What is that?" he whispered.

"It is Hí-no-no, the wind, mourning for his brother, the pine tree," but she would not tell him that tale, either. She went faster and faster, and Alan felt the stir of her shoulders under him. He listened to the wind, and it grew fierce and louder until he heard the house beams creak, for he was awake in his own bed. A strong wind drove gustily across the mesa and laid hold of the corners of the roof.

The next morning the homesteader said that he must go to the campoodie and Alan might go with him. Alan was quite pleased, and said to his mother while she was getting him ready, "Do you know, I think Indians are a great deal better off as they are now."

"Why, yes," said his mother, smiling, "I think so, too."

THE STREAM THAT RAN AWAY

In a short and shallow cañon on the front of Oppapago running eastward toward the sun, one may find a clear brown stream called the creek of Piñon Pines. That is not because it is unusual to find piñon trees on Oppapago, but because there are so few of them in the cañon of the stream. There are all sorts higher up on the slopes, — long-leaved yellow pines, thimble cones, tamarack, silver fir and Douglas spruce; but there is only a group of the low-heading, gray nut pines which the earliest inhabitants of the country called piñons.

The cañon of Piñon Pines has a pleasant outlook and lies open to the sun, but there is not much other cause for the forest rangers to remember it. At the upper end there is no more room by the stream border than will serve for a cattle trail; willows grow in it, choking the path of the water; there are brown birches here and ropes of white clematis tangled over thickets of brier rose. Low down the ravine broadens out to inclose a meadow the width of a lark's flight, blossomy and wet and good. Here the stream ran once in a maze of soddy banks and watered all the ground, and afterward ran out at the cañon's mouth across the mesa in a wash of bone-white boulders as far as it could. That was not very far, for it was a slender stream. It had its source really on the high crests and hollows of Oppapago, in the snow banks that melted and seeped downward through

16

the rocks; but the stream did not know any more of that than you know of what happened to you before you were born, and could give no account of itself except that it crept out from under a great heap of rubble far up in the cañon of Piñon Pines. And because it had no pools in it deep enough for trout, and no trees on its borders but gray nut pines; because, try as it might, it could never get across the mesa to the town, the stream had fully made up its mind to run away.

"Pray what good will that do you?" said the pines. "If you get to the town, they will turn you into an irrigating ditch and set you to watering crops."

"As to that," said the stream, "if I once get started I will not stop at the town." Then it would fret between its banks until the spangled fills of the mimulus were all tattered with its spray. Often at the end of the summer it was worn quite thin and small with running, and not able to do more than reach the meadow.

"But some day," it whispered to the stones, "I shall run quite away."

If the stream had been inclined for it, there was no lack of good company on its own borders. Birds nested in the willows, rabbits came to drink; one summer a bobcat made its lair up the bank opposite the brown birches and often deer fed in the meadow. Then there was a promise of better things. In the spring of one year two old men came up into the cañon of Piñon Pines. They had been miners and partners together for many years, they had grown rich and grown poor, and had seen many hard places and strange times. It was a day when the creek ran clear and the south wind smelled of the earth. Wild bees began to whine among the willows, and the meadow bloomed over the poppy-breasted larks. Then said one of the old men, "Here is

17

good meadow and water enough; let us build a house and grow trees. We are too old to dig in the mines."

"Let us set about it," said the other; for that is the way with two who have been a long time together: what one thinks of, the other is for doing. So they brought their possessions and made a beginning that day, for they felt the spring come on warmly in their blood; they wished to dig in the earth and handle it.

These two men who, in the mining camps where they were known, were called "Shorty" and "Long Tom," and had almost forgotten that they had other names, built a house by the water border and planted trees. Shorty was all for an orchard, but Long Tom preferred vegetables. So they did each what he liked, and were never so happy as when walking in the garden in the cool of the day, touching the growing things as they walked and praising each other's work.

"This will make a good home for our old age," said Long Tom, "and when we die we can be buried here."

"Under the piñon pines," said Shorty. "I have marked out a place."

So they were very happy for three years. By this time the stream had become so interested it had almost forgotten about running away. But every year it noted that a larger bit of the meadow was turned under and planted, and more and more the men made dams and ditches to govern its running.

"In fact," said the stream, "I am being made into an irrigating ditch before I have had my fling in the world. I really must make a start."

That very winter by the help of a great storm it went roaring down the meadow over the mesa, and so clean away, with only a track of muddy sand to show the way it had gone. All the winter, however, Shorty and Long Tom brought water for drinking from a spring and looked for the stream to come back. In the spring they hoped still, for that was the season they looked for the orchard to bear. But no fruit set on the trees, and the seeds Long Tom planted shriveled in the earth. So by the end of summer, when they understood that the water would not come back at all, they went sadly away.

Now what happened to the creek of Piñon Pines is not very well known to any one, for the stream is not very clear on that point, except that it did not have a happy time. It went out in the world on the wings of the storm and was very much tossed about and mixed up with other water, lost and bewildered. Everywhere it saw water at work, turning mills, watering fields, carrying trade, falling as hail, rain, and snow, and at the last, after many journeys, found itself creeping out from under the rocks of Oppapago in the cañon of Piñon Pines. Immediately the little stream knew itself and recalled clearly all that had happened to it before.

"After all, home is best," said the stream, and ran about in its choked channels looking for old friends. The willows were there, but grown shabby and dying at the top; the birches were quite dead, but stood still in their places; and there was only rubbish where the white clematis had been. Even the rabbits had gone away. The little stream ran whimpering in the meadow, fumbling at the ruined ditches to comfort the fruit-trees which were not quite dead. It was very dull in those days living in the cañon of Piñon Pines.

"But it is really my own fault," said the stream. So it went on repairing the borders with the best heart it could contrive.

About that time the white clematis had come back to hide the ruin of the brown birches, a young man came and camped with his wife and child in the meadow. They were looking for a place to make a home. They looked long at the meadow, for Shorty and Long Tom had taken away their home and it did not appear to belong to anyone.

"What a charming place!" said the young wife, "just the right distance from town, and a stream all to ourselves. And look, there are fruit-trees already planted. Do let us decide to stay."

Then she took off the child's shoes and stockings to let it play in the stream. The water curled all about the bare feet and gurgled delightedly.

"Ah, do stay," begged the happy water, "I can be such a help to you, for I know how a garden should be irrigated in the best manner."

The child laughed and stamped the water up to his bare knees. The young wife watched anxiously while her husband walked up and down the stream border and examined the fruit-trees.

"It is a delightful place," he said, "and the soil is rich, but I am afraid the water cannot be depended upon. There are signs of a great drought within the last two or three years. Look, there is a clump of birches in the very path of the stream, but all dead; and the largest limbs of the fruit-trees have died. In this country one must be able to make sure of the water supply. I suppose the people who planted them must have abandoned the place when the stream went dry. We must go on farther." So they took their goods and the child and went on farther.

"Ah, well," said the stream, "that is what is to be expected when one has a reputation for neglecting one's duty. But I wish they had stayed. That baby and I understood each other."

He had quite made up his mind not to run away again, though he could not be expected to be quite cheerful after all that had happened; in fact, if you go yourself to the cañon of the Piñon Pines you will notice that the stream, where it goes brokenly about the meadow, has quite a mournful sound.

THE COYOTE-SPIRIT
AND THE WEAVING WOMAN

The Weaving Woman lived under the bank of the stony wash that cut through the country of the mesquite dunes. The Coyote-Spirit, which, you understand, is an Indian whose form has been changed to fit with his evil behavior, ranged from the Black Rock where the wash began to the white sands beyond Pahranagat; and the Goat-Girl kept her flock among the mesquites, or along the windy stretch of sage below the campoodie; but as the Coyote-Spirit never came near the wickiups by day, and the Goat-Girl went home the moment the sun dropped behind Pahranagat, they never met. These three are all that have to do with the story.

The Weaving Woman, whose work was the making of fine baskets of split willow and roots of yucca and brown grass, lived alone, because there was nobody found who wished to live with her, and because it was whispered among the wickiups that she was different from other people. It was reported that she had an infirmity of the eyes which caused her to see everything with rainbow fringes, bigger and brighter and better than it was. All her days were fruitful, a handful of pine nuts as much to make merry over as a feast; every lad who went by a-hunting with his bow at his back looked to be a painted brave, and every old woman digging roots as fine as a medicine man in all his feathers. All the faces at the campoodie, dark as the mingled

22

sand and lava of the Black Rock country, deep lined with work and weather, shone for this singular old woman with the glory of the late evening light on Pahranagat. The door of her wickiup opened toward the campoodie with the smoke going up from cheerful hearths, and from the shadow of the bank where she sat to make baskets she looked down the stony wash where all the trails converged that led every way among the dunes, and saw an enchanted mesa covered with misty bloom and gentle creatures moving on trails that seemed to lead to the places where one had always wished to be.

Since all this was so, it was not surprising that her baskets turned out to be such wonderful affairs, and the tribesmen, though they winked and wagged their beads, were very glad to buy them for a haunch of venison or a bagful of mesquite meal. Sometimes, as they stroked the perfect curves of the bowls or traced out the patterns, they were heard to sigh, thinking how fine life would be if it were so rich and bright as she made it seem, instead of the dull occasion they had found it. There were some who even said it was a pity, since she was so clever at the craft, that the weaver was not more like other people, and no one thought to suggest that in that case her weaving would be no better than theirs. For all this the basket-maker did not care, sitting always happily at her weaving or wandering far into the desert in search of withes and barks and dyes, where the wild things showed her many a wonder hid from those who have not rainbow fringes to their eyes; and because she was not afraid of anything, she went farther and farther into the silent places until in the course of time she met the Coyote-Spirit.

Now a Coyote-Spirit, from having been a man, is continually thinking about men and wishing to be with them, and, being a coyote and of the wolf's breed, no sooner does he have his wish than he thinks of devouring. So as soon as this one had met the Weaving Woman he desired to eat her up, or to work her some evil according to the evil of his nature. He did not see any opportunity to begin at the first meeting, for on account of the infirmity of her eyes the woman did not see him as a coyote, but as a man, and let down her wicker water bottle for him to drink, so kindly that he was quite abashed. She did not seem in the least afraid of him, which is disconcerting even to a real coyote; though if he had been, she need not have been afraid of him in any case. Whatever pestiferous beast the Indian may think the dog of the wilderness, he has no reason to fear him except when by certain signs, as having a larger and leaner body, a sharper muzzle, and more evilly pointed ears, he knows him the soul of a bad-hearted man going about in that guise. There are enough of these coyote-spirits ranging in Mesquite Valley and over towards Funeral Mountains and about Pahranagat to give certain learned folk surmise as to whether there may not be a strange breed of wolves in that region; but the Indians know better.

When the coyote-spirit who had met the basket woman thought about it afterward, he said to himself that she deserved all the mischance that might come upon her for that meeting. "She knows," he said, "that this is my range, and whoever walks in a coyote-spirit's range must expect to take the consequences. She is not at all like the Goat-Girl."

The Coyote-Spirit had often watched the Goat-Girl from the top of Pahranagat, but because she was always in the open where no lurking-places were, and never far from the corn lands where the old men might be working, he had made himself believe he would not like that kind of a girl. Every morning he saw her come out of her leafy hut, loose the goats from the corral, which was all of cactus stems and broad leaves of prickly-pear, and lead them out among the wind-blown hillocks of sand under which the trunks of the mesquite flourished for a hundred years, and out of the tops of which the green twigs bore leaves and fruit; or along the mesa to browse on bitterbrush and the tops of scrubby sage. Sometimes she plaited willows for the coarser kinds of basketwork, or, in hot noonings, while the flock dozed, worked herself collars and necklaces of white and red and turquoise-colored beads, and other times sat dreaming on the sand. But whatever she did, she kept far enough from the place of the Coyote-Spirit, who, now that he had met the Weaving Woman, could not keep his mind off her. Her hut was far enough from the campoodie so that every morning he went around by the Black Rock to see if she was still there, and there she sat weaving patterns in her baskets of all that she saw or thought. Now it would be the winding wash and the wattled huts beside it, now the mottled skin of the rattlesnake or the curled plumes of the quail.

At last the Coyote-Spirit grew so bold that when there was no one passing on the trail he would go and walk up and down in front of the wickiup. Then the Weaving Woman would look up from her work and give him the news of the season and the tribesmen in so friendly a fashion that he grew less and less troubled in his mind about working her mischief. He said in his evil heart that since the ways of such as he were known to the Indians,—as indeed they were, with many a charm and spell to keep them safe,—it could be no fault of his if they came to harm through too much familiarity. As for the Weaving Woman, he said, "She sees me as I am, and ought to know better," for he had not heard about the infirmity of her eyes.

25

Finally he made up his mind to ask her to go with him to dig for roots around the foot of Pahranagat, and if she consented,— and of course she did, for she was a friendly soul,—he knew in his heart what he would do. They went out by the mesa trail, and it was a soft and blossomy day of spring. Long wands of the creosote with shining fretted foliage were hung with creamy bells of bloom, and doves called softly from the Dripping Spring. They passed rows of owlets sitting by their burrows and saw young rabbits playing in their shallow forms. The Weaving Woman talked gayly as they went, as Indian women talk, with soft mellow voices and laughter breaking in between the words like smooth water flowing over stones. She talked of how the deer had shifted their feeding grounds and of whether the quail had mated early that year as a sign of a good season, matters of which the Coyote-Spirit knew more than she, only he was not thinking of those things just then. Whenever her back was turned he licked his cruel jaws and whetted his appetite. They passed the level mesa, passed the tumbled fragments of the Black Rock and came to the sharp wall-sided cañons that showed the stars at noon from their deep wells of sombre shade, where no wild creature made its home and no birds ever sang. Then the Weaving Woman grew still at last because of the great stillness, and the Coyote-Spirit said in a hungry, whining voice,—

"Do you know why I brought you here?"

"To show me how still and beautiful the world is here," said the Weaving Woman, and even then she did not seem afraid.

"To eat you up," said the Coyote. With that he looked to see her fall quaking at his feet, and he had it in mind to tell her it was no fault but her own for coming so far astray with one of his kind, but the woman only looked at him and laughed. The sound of her laughter was like water in a bubbling spring.

"Why do you laugh?" said the Coyote, and he was so astonished that his jaws remained open when he had done speaking.

"How could you eat me?" said she. "Only wild beasts could do that."

"What am I, then?"

"Oh, you are only a man."

"I am a coyote," said he.

"Do you think I have no eyes?" said the woman. "Come!" For she did not understand that her eyes were different from other people's, what she really thought was that other people's were different from hers, which is quite another matter, so she pulled the Coyote-Spirit over to a rain-fed pool. In that country the rains collect in basins of the solid rock that grow polished with a thousand years of storm and give back from their shining side a reflection like a mirror. One such lay in the bottom of the black cañon, and the Weaving Woman stood beside it.

Now it is true of coyote-spirits that they are so only because of their behavior; not only have they power to turn themselves to men if they wish—but they do not wish, or they would not have become coyotes in the first place—but other people in their company, according as they think man-thoughts or beast-thoughts, can throw over them such a change that they have only to choose which they will be. So the basket-weaver contrived to throw the veil of her mind over the Coyote-Spirit, so that when he looked at himself in the pool he could not tell for the life of him whether he was most coyote or most man, which so frightened him that he ran away and left the Weaving Woman to hunt for roots alone. He ran for three days and nights, being afraid of himself, which is the worst possible fear, and then ran

27

back to see if the basket-maker had not changed her mind. He put his head in at the door of her wickiup.

"Tell me, now, am I a coyote or a man?"

"Oh, a man," said she, and he went off to Pahranagat to think it over. In a day or two he came back.

"And what now?" he said.

"Oh, a man, and I think you grow handsomer every day."

That was really true, for what with her insisting upon it and his thinking about it, the beast began to go out of him and the man to come back. That night he went down to the campoodie to try and steal a kid from the corral, but it occurred to him just in time that a man would not do that, so he went back to Pahranagat and ate roots and berries instead, which was a true sign that he had grown into a man again. Then there came a day when the Weaving Woman asked him to stop at her hearth and eat. There was a savory smell going up from the cooking-pots, cakes of mesquite meal baking in the ashes, and sugary white buds of the yucca palm roasting on the coals. The man who had been a coyote lay on a blanket of rabbit skin and heard the cheerful snapping of the fire. It was all so comfortable and bright that somehow it made him think of the Goat-Girl.

"That is the right sort of a girl," he said to himself. "She has always stayed in the safe open places and gone home early. She should be able to tell me what I am," for he was not quite sure, and since he had begun to walk with men a little, he had heard about the Weaving Woman's eyes.

Next day he went out where the flock fed, not far from the corn lands, and the Goat-Girl did not seem in the least afraid of him. So he went again, and the third day he said,—

"Tell me what I seem to you."

28

"A very handsome man," said she.

"Then will you marry me?" said he; and when the Goat-Girl had taken time to think about it she said yes, she thought she would.

Now, when the man who had been a coyote lay on the blanket of the Weaving Woman's wickiup, he had taken notice how it was made of willows driven into the ground around a pit dug in the earth, and the poles drawn together at the top, and thatched with brush, and he had tried at the foot of Pahranagat until he had built another like it; so when he had married the Goat-Girl, after the fashion of her tribe, he took her there to live. He was not now afraid of anything except that his wife might get to know that he had once been a coyote. It was during the first month of their marriage that he said to her, "Do you know the basket-maker who lives under the bank of the stony wash? They call her the Weaving Woman."

"I have heard something of her and I have bought her baskets. Why do you ask?"

"It is nothing," said the man, "but I hear strange stories of her, that she associates with coyote-spirits and such creatures," for he wanted to see what his wife would say to that.

"If that is the case," said she, "the less we see of her the better. One cannot be too careful in such matters."

After that, when the man who had been a coyote and his wife visited the campoodie, they turned out of the stony wash before they reached the wickiup, and came in to the camp by another trail. But I have not heard whether the Weaving Woman noticed it.

THE CHEERFUL GLACIER

Very many years ago, at the foot of a nameless peak between Mount Ritter and Togobah, after three successive years of deep snow there was a glacier born. It crept out fanwise from a furrow on the mountain-side, very high up, above the limit of the white-barked pines, and its upper end was lost under the drift of loose snow that trailed down the slope. For three successive winters the gray veil of storms hung month-long about the crest of the Sierras, while the snow came falling, falling, and the wind kept heaping, heaping, until the drifts sagged and slipped of their own weight down the long groove of the mountain; and since it lay on the sunless northern slope, and as it happened the summers that came between fell cool and rainy, there, when the spring thaw had cleared the loose snow, spread out on a little stony flat lay the rim of the glacier. Yet it was a very little one, a rod or two of clear shining ice that ran into deep blue and gray sludge under a drift of coarse, whitish granules, and very high up, fine dry particles of snow like powdered glass. So it lay at the time of year when the mountain sheep began to come back to their summer feeding-grounds.

When the thaw had cleared the heather and warmed the lichened rocks, they loosed their hold of the ice, and the great weight of it began to crawl down the mountain. At the first slow thrill of motion the little glacier creaked with delight.

"Ah," it said, "it is evident that I am not a mere snow bank, for in that case I should remain in one place. Now I know myself truly a glacier." For up to that time it had been in some doubt.

By the end of the summer it had advanced more than a span in the shadow of the peak. Then the snows began, deep and heavy, but the glacier did not complain; it hugged the floor of the rift where it lay, and thought of the time when it should start on its travels again. So, because of thinking about it so much, or because the snows were deeper and the summers not so warm, the glacier increased and went forward until it had quite crossed the stony flat, and began to believe it might make its mark in the world. There were any number of reasons for thinking so. To begin with, all that neighborhood was deeply scarred and scoured by the trail of old glaciers, and the high peaks glittered with the keen polish of ice floes. All down the slope shone glassy bosses of clear granite succeeding to beds of cassiope and blue heather, polished slips of granite, pentstemon and more heather, smooth granite that the feet could take no hold upon, then saxifrage and meadowsweet, and so down to the stream border, where the water quarreled with the stones. And by the time the little glacier had settled that it would leave such a mark on the mountain-side, shining and softened by small blossomy things, it had come quite to the farthest border of the flat, and looked over the edge of a sharp descent. It was much too far to bend over, for though the glacier was all of brittle ice, it could bend a little.

"But it is really nothing," said the glacier. "I have only to grind down the cliff until it is the proper height;" and it took a firmer hold on the sharp fragments of stones it had gathered on its way down the ravine. The pressure of the sodden snow above kept on, however, and before the glacier had fairly begun its grinding the ice rim was pushed out beyond the bluff, broke off, and lay at the foot in a shining heap.

"So much the better," said the cheerful glacier. "What with grinding above and filling with broken ice below, the work will be accomplished in half the time."

But that never really happened, for this was the last season the ice reached to the far edge of the flat. The next year there was less snow and more sun. The long slope of bare rocks gathered up the heat and held it so that the ice began to melt underneath, and a stream ran from it and fell over the cliff in a fine silvery veil.

"How very fortunate," said the glacier, "to become the head of a river so early in my career. Besides, this is a much easier way of getting over the falls."

Then the water began to purr in sheer content where it went among the stones; it increased and went down the cañon toward the white torrent of the creek that flowed from Togobah, and the next summer a water ousel found it. She came whirling up the course of the stream like a thrown pebble, plump and slaty blue, scattering a spray of sound as clear and round as the trickle of ice water that went over the falls. The ousel sat on the edge of the ice rim to finish her song, and it timed with the running of the stream.

"You should understand," said the glacier, "that I started in life with the intention of cutting my way down the mountain. But now I am a river I am quite as well pleased."

"Everything is the best," said the ousel; "that has been the motto of my family for a long time, and I am sure I have proved it." And if one listened close as she flew in and out of the falls and sought in the white torrent for her food, one understood that it was the burden of her song. "Everything is the best," she sang, and kept on singing it when the glacier had grown so small by running that it was quite hollowed out under the roof of granulated snow, and the light came through it softly and wonderfully blue. Then the ousel would go far up into this ice cave until the sound of her singing came out wild and sweet, mixed with the water and the tinkle of the ice. As for the words of her song, the glacier never disagreed with her, though by now it had retreated clear across its stony flat. But the wind brought in the seeds of dwarf willow that sprouted and took root, and bright little buttercups began to come up and shiver in the flood of ice water.

"It seems I am to have a meadow of my own," said the glacier, by the time there was stone-crop and purple pentstemon blowing in the damp crevices about its border. "I do not believe there is a prettier ice garden on this side of the mountain. And to think that all I once wished was to leave a track of bare and shining stones! The ousel is right, everything is for the best."

The ousel always went downstream at the beginning of the winter, when the running waters were shut under snow bridges and the pools were puddles of gray sludge, down and down to the foothill borders, and at the turn of the year followed up again in the wake of the thaw. So it was not often that the ousel and the glacier saw each other between October and June.

"But of course," said the glacier, "the longer you are away, the more we have to say to each other when you come."

"And anyway it cannot be helped," said the ousel. For though she did not mind the storms and cold weather, one cannot really exist without eating.

After one of these winter trips, the ousel noticed that the

stream that came over the fall had quite failed, ran only a slender trickle that dripped among the shivering fern and was lost in the rock crevices, and though she was such a cheerful little body, she did not like to be the first to speak of it. It seemed as if the glacier could not last much longer at that rate. So she flitted about in the lacework caverns of the ice, and sang airily and sweet, and the words of her song were what they had always been.

"That is quite true," said the glacier. "You see how it is with me; once I was very proud to run over the fall with a splashing sound, but now I find it better to keep all the water for my meadow."

In fact, there was quite a border of sod all about where the ice had been, and a great mat of white-belled cassiope in the middle. It grew greener and more blossomy every year. The ousel grew so used to finding it there, and so pleased with the society of the glacier, which was quite after her own heart, that it was a great grief to her as she came whirling up the stream in the flood tide of the year to find that they had both, the meadow and the ice, wholly disappeared.

That had been a winter of long, thunderous storms, and a great splinter of granite had fallen away from the mountain peaks and slid down in a heap of rubble over the place where the glacier had been. There was now no trace of it under sharp, broken stones.

But because they had been friends, the ousel could not keep quite away from the place, but came again and again and flew chirruping around the foot of the hill. One of those days when the sun was strong and the heather white on the wild headlands, she saw a slender rill of water creeping out at the bottom of the rubbish heap, and knew at once by the cheerful sound of it that it must be her friend the glacier, or what was left of it.

"Yes, indeed," bubbled the spring, "it is really surprising what good luck I have. As a glacier, I suppose I should have quite melted away in a few summers; but with all this protection of loose stones, I should n't wonder if I became a perennial spring."

And in fact that is exactly what occurred, for with the snow that sifted down between the broken boulders, and the snow water that collected in the hollow where the meadow had been, the spring has never gone quite dry. Every summer, when the heather and pentstemon and saxifrage on the glacier slip are at their best, the cheerful water comes out of the foot of the nameless peak and the ousel comes up from the white torrent and sits upon the stones. Then they sing together, and their voices blend perfectly; but if you listen carefully, you will observe that the words of their song are always the same.

THE MERRY-GO-ROUND

The Basket Woman was washing for the homesteader's wife at the spring, and Alan, by this time very good friends with her, was pulling up sagebrush for the fire, when the coyote came by. It was a clear, wide morning, warm and sweet, with gusty flaws of cooler air moving down from Pine Mountain. There was a lake of purple lupins in the swale, and the last faint flush of wild almonds burning on the slope. The grapevines at the spring were full of bloom and tender leaf. Eastward, above the high tilted mesa under the open sky, the buzzards were making a merry-go-round. That was the way Alan always thought of their performance when he saw them circling slantwise under the sun. Round and round they went, now so low that he could see how the shabby wing feathers frayed out at the edges, now so high that they became mere specks against the sky.

"What makes them go round and round?" asked Alan of the mahala.

"They go about to wait for their dinner, but the table is not yet spread," said she. The Basket Woman did not use quite such good English; but though Alan understood her broken talk, you probably would not. The little boy could not imagine, though he tried, what a buzzard's dinner might be like. The high mesa, with the water of mirage rolling over it, was a kind of enchanted land to him where almost anything might happen. He would

36

lie contentedly for hours with his head pillowed on the hillocks
of blown sand about the roots of the sage, and look up at the
merry-go-round. He noticed that, although others joined them
from the invisible upper sky, none ever seemed to go away, but
hung and circled and faded into the thin blue deeps of air. Often
he saw them settle flockwise below the rim of the mesa and beyond his sight, wondering greatly what they might be about.

The morning at the spring he watched them in the intervals
of tending the sagebrush fire, and then it was that the coyote
came by, going in that direction. His head was cocked to one
side, and he seemed to watch the merry-go-round out of the
corner of his eye as he went.

Alan thought the little gray beast had not seen them at the
spring, but in that he was mistaken. A quarter of an hour before, as he came up out of the gully that hid his lair, the coyote
had sighted the boy and the Basket Woman and made sure in
his own mind that they had no gun. So, as it lay in his way, he
came quite close to them; opposite the spring he paused a moment with one foot lifted, and eyed them with a wise and secret
look. He went on toward the mesa, stopped again, looked back
and then up at the whirling buzzards, and went on again.

"Where does that one go?" asked Alan.

"Eh," said the Basket Woman, "he goes also to the dinner. It
is good eating they have out there on the mesa together."

Alan looked after him, and the coyote paused and looked back
over his shoulder as one who expects to be followed, and quite
suddenly it came into the boy's mind to go up on the mesa and
see what it was all about. The Basket Woman was bent above
her tubs and did not see him go; when she missed him she supposed he had gone back to the house. Alan trotted on after the

coyote until he lost him in a sunken place full of boulders and black sage; but he had been headed still toward that spot above which the black wings beat dizzily, and that way Alan went, climbing by the help of stout shrubs to the mesa, which here fell off steeply to the valley, and then on until he saw his coyote or another one, going steadily toward the merry-go-round.

The mesa was very warm, and swam in misty blueness although the day was clear. Dim shapes of mountains stood up on the far edge, and near by a procession of lonely, low hills rounded like the backs of dolphins appearing out of the sea. Stubby shrubs as tall as Alan's shoulder covered the mesa sparingly, and in wide spaces there were beds of yellow-flowered prickly-pear; singly and far stood up tall stems of white-belled yucca, called in that country Candles of Our Lord. Alan could not follow the coyote close among the scrub, but dropped presently into a cattle trail that ran toward the place where he supposed the coyote's dinner must be, and so trudged on in it while the sun wheeled high in the heavens and the whole air of the mesa quivered with the heat.

It is certain that in his wanderings Alan must have traveled that day and the next as much as twenty miles from the spring, though he might easily have been lost in less time, for his head hardly came above the tops of the scrub, and there were no landmarks to guide by, other than the low hills which seemed to alter nothing whichever way one looked at them. As for the buzzards, they rose higher and higher into the dim, quivering air. Alan began to be thirsty, next tired, and then hungry. He tried to turn toward home, but got no nearer, and finally understood that he might be lost, so he ran about wildly for a time, which made matters no better. He began to cry and to run eagerly at the same time until, blind and breathless, he would fall and lie sobbing, and wish that he might see his mother or the Basket Woman come walking across the mesa with her basket on her back. By this time it was hot and close and he had come where the scant-leaved shrubs were far between, and with heat and running the tears were dried out of him. He sobbed in his breath and his lips were cracked and dry. It fell cooler as night drew on, but he grew sick with hunger, and shuddered with the fear of darkness. Far off across the mesa the coyotes began to howl.

Down in the homesteader's cabin nobody slept that night. When they first missed Alan, which was at noon, no one had the least idea where he was. His mother had supposed him at the spring, and the Basket Woman thought he had gone to his mother. It was all open ground about the cabin from the mesa and the foot of the hills, and below it toward the valley bare stretches of moon-white sands.

The homesteader thought that the boy might have gone to the campoodie; but there they found he had not been, and none of the Indians had seen him; but by three of the clock they were all out beating about the spring to pick up the light trail of his feet, and there they were when the quick dark came on and stopped them.

By the earliest light of the next morning the Basket Woman, who was really very fond of him, had come out of her hut to ask for news, but when she had looked up to the sky for a token of what the day was to be, she saw the buzzards come slantwise out of space and begin the merry-go-round. All at once she remembered Alan's question of the day before, and though she could not reasonably expect any one to take any notice of it, an idea came into her head and a gleam into her beady eyes. She caught her pony from the corral, riding him astride as Indian women ride, with the wicker water bottle slung across her shoulder and a parcel of food hid in her bosom. She went up the mesa rim toward the spot where the buzzards swung circling in the sky.

When Alan awoke that morning under the creosote bush, he thought he must have come nearly to the place he had meant to find the day before. There was the coyote skulking out in the cactus scrub, and the buzzards wheeling low and large. It was a hot, smoky morning, the soil was all of coarse gravel, loose and white. Over to the right of him lay a still blue pool, and a broad river flowed into it in soft billows without sound. The coyote went toward it, looking back over his shoulder, and Alan followed, for his tongue was swollen in his mouth with thirst. The little boy was quite clear in his mind; he knew that he was lost, that he was very hungry, and that it was necessary to find his father and mother very soon. As he had come toward the mountains the day before, he thought that he should start directly away from them. He thought he could not be far from the campoodie, for it came to him dimly that he had heard the Indians singing the coyote song in the night, but he meant to have a drink in the soft still billows of the stream. A little ahead of him the coyote seemed to have gone into it, his head just cleared the surface, and the water heaved to the movements of his shoulders. But somehow Alan got no nearer to it. The stream seemed to loop and curve away from him, and presently he saw the lake behind him and could not think how that could be, for he did not understand that it was a lake and river of mirage. He saw the trees stand up on its borders, and fancied that the air which came from it was moist and cool. Always the coyote went before and showed him the way, and at last he lifted up his long thin muzzle and made a doleful cry. Mostly it seemed to Alan that the coyotes howled like dogs, but a little crazily; now it appeared that this one spoke in words that he could understand. When he told his mother of it afterwards, she said it was only the fever of his thirst and fatigue, but the Basket Woman believed him.

"Ho, ho!" cried the coyote, "come, come, my brothers, to the hunting! Come!"

A great black shadow of wings fell over them and a voice cried huskily, "What of the quarry?"

"The quarry is close at hand," said the coyote, and Alan wondered dizzily what they might be talking about. He could not look up, for his eyes were nearly blinded by the light that beat up from the sand, but he saw wing shadows thickening on the ground.

"Where do you go now?" cried the voice in the upper air.

"Round and about to the false water until he is very weary," said the coyote; and it seemed to Alan that he must follow where the gray dog went in a maze of moving shadows. He trembled and fell from weakness a great many times and lay with his face in the shelter of the prickle bushes, but always he got up and went on again.

"Have a care," cried the voice in the air, "here comes one of his own kind."

"What and where?" said the coyote.

"It is a brown one riding on a horse; she comes up from the gully of big rocks."

"Does she follow a trail?" panted the coyote.

"She follows no trail, but rides fast in this direction," croaked the voice, but Alan took no interest in it. He did not know that it was the Basket Woman coming to rescue him. He thought of the merry-go-round, for he saw that he had come back to the creosote bush where he had spent the night, and he thought the earth had come round with him, for it rocked and reeled as he went. His tongue hung out of his mouth and his lips cracked and bled, his feet were blistered and aching from the sharp rocks, the hot sands, and cactus thorns. Round and round with him went scrub and sand, on one side the shadow of black wings, and on the other the smooth flow of mirage water which he might never reach. Through it all he could hear the soft *biff, biff* of the broad wings and the long, hungry, whining howl that seemed to detach itself from any throat and come upon him from all quarters of the quivering air. Dizzily went the merry-go-round, and now it seemed that the false water swung nearer, that it went around with him, that it bore him up, for he no longer felt the earth under him, that it buoyed and floated him far out from the place where he had been, that it grew deliciously cool at last, that it laved his face and flowed in his parched throat; and at last he opened his eyes and found the Basket Woman trickling water in his mouth from her wicker water bottle. It was noon of his second day from home when she found him on Cactus Flat, by going straight to the point where she saw the black wings hanging in the air. She laid him on the horse before her and dripped water in his mouth and coaxed and called to him, but never left off riding nor halted until she came up with others of the search party who had followed up by the place where Alan had climbed to the mesa, and followed slowly by a faint trail. But to Alan it was all as if he had dreamed that the Basket Woman had brought him as before from the valley of Corn Water. The first that he realized was that his father had him, and that his mother was crying and kissing the Basket Woman. It was several days before he was able to be about again, and then only under promise that he would go no farther than the spring. The first thing he saw when he looked up was the buzzards high up over the mesa making a merry-go-round in the clear blue, and it was then he remembered that he had not yet found out what it was all about.

THE CHRISTMAS TREE

Eastward from the Sierras rises a strong red hill known as Pine Mountain, though the Indians call it The Hill of Summer Snow. At its foot stands a town of a hundred board houses, given over wholly to the business of mining. The noise of it goes on by day and night, — the creak of the windlasses, the growl of the stamps in the mill, the clank of the cars running down to the dump, and from the open doors of the drinking saloons, great gusts of laughter and the sound of singing. Billows of smoke roll up from the tall stacks and by night are lit ruddily by the smelter fires all going at a roaring blast.

Whenever the charcoal-burner's son looked down on the red smoke, the glare, and the hot breath of the furnaces, it seemed to him like an exhalation from the wickedness that went on continually in the town; though all he knew of wickedness was the word, a rumor from passers-by, and a kind of childish fear. The charcoal-burner's cabin stood on a spur of Pine Mountain two thousand feet above the town, and sometimes the boy went down to it on the back of the laden burros when his father carried charcoal to the furnaces. All else that he knew were the wild creatures of the mountain, the trees, the storms, the small flowering things, and away at the back of his heart a pale memory of his mother like the faint forest odor that clung to the black embers of the pine. They had lived in the town when the mother was alive and the father worked in the mines. There were not many women or children in the town at that time, but mining men jostling with rude quick ways; and the young mother was not happy.

"Never let my boy grow up in such a place," she said as she lay dying; and when they had buried her in the coarse shallow soil, her husband looked for comfort up toward The Hill of Summer Snow shining purely, clear white and quiet in the sun. It swam in the upper air above the sooty reek of the town and seemed as if it called. Then he took the young child up to the mountain, built a cabin under the tamarack pines, and a pit for burning charcoal for the furnace fires.

No one could wish for a better place for a boy to grow up in than the slope of Pine Mountain. There was the drip of pine balm and a wind like wine, white water in the springs, and as much room for roaming as one desired. The charcoal-burner's son chose to go far, coming back with sheaves of strange bloom from the edge of snow banks on the high ridges, bright spar or peacock-painted ores, hatfuls of berries, or strings of shining trout. He played away whole mornings in glacier meadows where he heard the eagle scream; walking sometimes in a mist of cloud he came upon deer feeding, or waked them from their lair in the deep fern. On snow-shoes in winter he went over the deep drifts and spied among the pine tops on the sparrows, the grouse, and the chilly robins wintering under the green tents. The deep snow lifted him up and held him among the second stories of the trees. But that was not until he was a great lad, straight and springy as a young fir. As a little fellow he spent his days at the end of a long rope staked to a pine just out of reach of the choppers and the charcoal-pits. When he was able to go about alone, his father made him give three promises: never to follow a bear's trail nor meddle with the cubs, never to try to climb the eagle rocks after the young eagles, never to lie down nor to sleep on the sunny, south slope where the rattlesnakes frequented. After that he was free of the whole wood.

When Mathew, for so the boy was called, was ten years old, he began to be of use about the charcoal-pits, to mark the trees for cutting, to sack the coals, to keep the house, and cook his father's meals. He had no companions of his own age nor wanted any, for at this time he loved the silver firs. A group of them grew in a swale below the cabin, tall and fine; the earth under them was slippery and brown with needles. Where they stood close together with overlapping boughs the light among the tops was golden green, but between the naked boles it was a vapor thin and blue. These were the old trees that had wagged their tops together for three hundred years. Around them stood a ring of saplings and seedlings scattered there by the parent firs, and a little apart from these was the one that Mathew loved. It was slender of trunk and silvery white, the branches spread out fanwise to the outline of a perfect spire. In the spring, when the young growth covered it as with a gossamer web, it gave out a pleasant odor, and it was to him like the memory of what his mother had been. Then he garlanded it with flowers and hung streamers of white clematis all heavy with bloom upon its boughs. He brought it berries in cups of bark and sweet water from the spring; always as long as he knew it, it seemed to him that the fir tree had a soul.

The first trip he had ever made on snow-shoes was to see how it fared among the drifts. That was always a great day when he could find the slender cross of its topmost bough above the snow. The fir was not very tall in those days, but the snows as far down on the slope as the charcoal-burner's cabin lay shallowly. There was a time when Mathew expected to be as tall as the fir, but after a while the boy did not grow so fast and the fir kept on adding its whorl of young branches every year.

Mathew told it all his thoughts. When at times there was a heaviness in his breast which was really a longing for his mother, though he did not understand it, he would part the low spreading branches and creep up to the slender trunk of the fir. Then he would put his arms around it and be quiet for a long beautiful time. The tree had its own way of comforting him; the branches swept the ground and shut him in dark and close. He made a little cairn of stones under it and kept his treasures there.

Often as he sat snuggled up to the heart of the tree, the boy would slip his hand over the smooth intervals between the whorls of boughs, and wonder how they knew the way to grow. All the fir trees are alike in this, that they throw out their branches from the main stem like the rays of a star, one added to another with the season's growth. They stand out stiffly from the trunk, and the shape of each new bough in the beginning and the shape of the last growing twig when they have spread out broadly with many branchlets, bending with the weight of their own needles, is the shape of a cross; and the topmost sprig that rises above all the star-built whorls is a long and slender cross, until by the springing of new branches it becomes a star. So the two forms go on running into and repeating each other, and each star is like all the stars, and every bough is another's twin. It is this trim and certain growth that sets out the fir from all the mountain trees, and gives to the young saplings a secret look as they stand straight and stiffly among the wild brambles on the hill. For the wood delights to grow abroad at all points, and one might search a summer long without finding two leaves of the oak alike, or any two trumpets of the spangled mimulus. So, as at that time he had nothing better worth studying about, Mathew noticed and pondered the secret of the silver fir, and grew up with it until he was twelve years old and tall and strong for his age. By this time the charcoal-burner began to be troubled about the boy's schooling.

Meantime there was rioting and noise and coming and going of strangers in the town at the foot of Pine Mountain, and the furnace blast went on ruddily and smokily. Because of the things he heard Mathew was afraid, and on rare occasions when he went down to it he sat quietly among the charcoal sacks, and would not go far away from them except when he held his father by the hand. After a time, it seemed life went more quietly there, flowers began to grow in the yards of the houses, and they met children walking in the streets with books upon their arms.

"Where are they going, father?" said the boy.

"To school," said the charcoal-burner.

"And may I go?" asked Mathew.

"Not yet, my son."

But one day his father pointed out the foundations of a new building going up in the town.

"It is a church," he said, "and when that is finished it will be a sign that there will be women here like your mother, and then you may go to school."

Mathew ran and told the fir tree all about it.

"But I will never forget you, never," he cried, and he kissed the trunk. Day by day, from the spur of the mountain, he watched the church building, and it was wonderful how much he could see in that clear, thin atmosphere; no other building in town interested him so much. He saw the walls go up and the roof, and the spire rise skyward with something that glittered twinkling on its top. Then they painted the church white and hung a bell in the tower. Mathew fancied he could hear it of Sundays as he saw the people moving along like specks in the streets.

"Next week," said the father, "the school begins, and it is time for you to go as I promised. I will come to see you once a month, and when the term is over you shall come back to the mountain." Mathew said good-by to the fir tree, and there were tears in his eyes though he was happy. "I shall think of you very often," he said, "and wonder how you are getting along. When I come back I will tell you everything that happens. I will go to church, and I am sure I shall like that. It has a cross on top like yours, only it is yellow and shines. Perhaps when I am gone I shall learn why you carry a cross, also." Then he went a little timidly, holding fast by his father's hand.

There were so many people in the town that it was quite as strange and fearful to him as it would be to you who have grown up in town to be left alone in the wood. At night, when he saw the charcoal-burner's fires glowing up in the air where the bulk of the mountain melted into the dark, he would cry a little under the blankets, but after he began to learn, there was no more occasion for crying. It was to the child as though there had been a candle lighted in a dark room. On Sunday he went to the church, and then it was both light and music, for he heard the minister read about God in the great book and believed it all, for everything that happens in the woods is true, and people who grow up in it are best at believing. Mathew thought it was all as the minister said, that there is nothing better than pleasing God. Then when he lay awake at night he would try to think how it would have been with him if he had never come to this place. In his heart he began to be afraid of the time when he would have to go back to the mountain, where there was no one to tell him about this most important thing in the world, for his father never talked to him of these things. It preyed upon his mind, but if any one noticed it, they thought that he pined for his father and wished himself at home.

It drew toward midwinter, and the white cap on The Hill of Summer Snow, which never quite melted even in the warmest weather, began to spread downward until it reached the charcoal-burner's home. There was a great stir and excitement among the children, for it had been decided to have a Christmas tree in the church. Every Sunday now the Christ-child story was told over and grew near and brighter like the Christmas star. Mathew had not known about it before, except that on a certain day in the year his father had bought him toys. He had supposed that it was because it was stormy and he had to be indoors. Now he was wrapped up in the story of love and sacrifice, and felt his heart grow larger as he breathed it in, looking upon clear windless nights to see if he might discern the Star of Bethlehem rising over Pine Mountain and the Christ-child come walking on the snow. It was not that he really expected it, but that the story was so alive in him. It is easy for those who have lived long in the high mountains to believe in beautiful things. Mathew wished in his heart that he might never go away from this place. He sat in his seat in church, and all that the minister said sank deeply into his mind.

When it came time to decide about the tree, because Mathew's father was a charcoal-burner and knew where the best trees grew, it was quite natural to ask him to furnish the tree for his part. Mathew fairly glowed with delight, and his father was pleased, too, for he liked to have his son noticed. The Saturday before Christmas, which fell on Tuesday that year, was the time set for going for the tree, and by that time Mathew had quite settled in his mind that it should be his silver fir. He did not know how otherwise he could bring the tree to share in his new delight, nor what else he had worth giving, for he quite believed what he had been told, that it is only through giving the best beloved that one comes to the heart's desire. With all his heart Mathew wished never to live in any place where he might not hear about God. So when his father was ready with the ropes and the sharpened axe, the boy led the way to the silver firs.

"Why, that is a little beauty," said the charcoal-burner, "and just the right size."

They were obliged to shovel away the snow to get at it for cutting, and Mathew turned away his face when the chips began to fly. The tree fell upon its side with a shuddering sigh; little beads of clear resin stood out about the scar of the axe. It seemed as if the tree wept. But how graceful and trim it looked when it stood in the church waiting for gifts! Mathew hoped that it would understand.

The charcoal-burner came to church on Christmas eve, the first time in many years. It makes a difference about these things when you have a son to take part in them. The church and the tree were alight with candles; to the boy it seemed like what he supposed the place of dreams might be. One large candle burned on the top of the tree and threw out pointed rays like a star; it made the charcoal-burner's son think of Bethlehem. Then he heard the minister talking, and it was all of a cross and a star; but Mathew could only look at the tree, for he saw that it trembled, and he felt that he had betrayed it. Then the choir began to sing, and the candle on top of the tree burned down quite low, and Mathew saw the slender cross of the topmost bough stand up dark before it. Suddenly he remembered his old puzzle about it, how the smallest twigs were divided off in each in the shape of a cross, how the boughs repeated the star form every year, and what was true of his fir was true of them all. Then it must have been that there were tears in his eyes, for he could not see plainly: the pillars of the church spread upward like the shafts of the trees, and the organ playing was like the sound of the wind in their branches, and the stately star-built firs rose up like spires, taller than the church tower, each with a cross on top. The sapling which was still before him trembled more, moving its boughs as if it spoke; and the boy heard it in his heart and believed, for it spoke to him of God. Then all the fear went out of his heart and he had no more dread of going back to the mountain to spend his days, for now he knew that he need never be away from the green reminder of hope and sacrifice in the star and the cross of the silver fir; and the thought broadened in his mind that he might find more in the forest than he had ever thought to find, now that he knew what to look for, since everything speaks of God in its own way and it is only a matter of understanding how.

It was very gay in the little church that Christmas night, with laughter and bonbons flying about, and every child had a package of candy and an armful of gifts. The charcoal-burner had his pockets bulging full of toys, and Mathew's eyes glowed like the banked fires of the charcoal-pits as they walked home in the keen, windless night.

"Well, my boy," said the charcoal-burner, "I am afraid you will not be wanting to go back to the mountain with me after this."

"Oh, yes, I will," said Mathew happily, "for I think the mountains know quite as much of the important things as they know here in the town."

"Right you are," said the charcoal-burner, as he clapped his boy's hand between both his own, "and I am pleased to think you have turned out such a sensible little fellow." But he really did not know all that was in his son's heart.

THE FIRE BRINGER

This is one of the stories that Alan had from the Basket Woman after she came to understand that the boy really loved her tales and believed them. She would sit by the spring with her hands clasped across her knees while the clothes boiled and Alan fed the fire with broken brush, and tell him wonder stories as long as the time allowed, which was never so long as the boy liked to hear them. The story of the Fire Bringer gave him the greatest delight, and he made a game of it to play with little Indian boys from the campoodie who sometimes strayed in the direction of the homesteader's cabin. It was the story that came oftenest to his mind when he lay in his bed at night, and saw the stars in the windy sky shine through the cabin window.

He heard of it so often and thought of it so much that at last it seemed to him that he had been part of the story himself, but his mother said he must have dreamed it. The experience came to him in this way: He had gone with his father to the mountains for a load of wood, a two days' journey from home, and they had taken their blankets to sleep upon the ground, which was the first time of Alan's doing so. It was the time of year when white gilias, which the children call "evening snow," were in bloom, and their musky scent was mingled with the warm air in the soft dark all about him.

He heard the camp-fire snap and whisper, and saw the flicker of it brighten and die on the lower branches of the pines. He looked up and saw the stars in the deep velvet void, and now and then one fell from it, trailing all across the sky. Small winds moved in the tops of the sage and trod lightly in the dark, blossomy grass. Near by them ran a flooding creek, the sound of it among the stones like low-toned, cheerful talk. Familiar voices seemed to rise through it and approach distinctness. The boy lay in his blanket harking to one recurring note, until quite suddenly it separated itself from the babble and called to him in the Basket Woman's voice. He was sure it was she who spoke his name, though he could not see her; and got up on his feet at once. He knew, too, that he was Alan, and yet it seemed, without seeming strange, that he was the boy of the story who was afterward to be called the Fire Bringer. The skin of his body was dark and shining, with straight, black locks cropped at his shoulders, and he wore no clothing but a scrap of deerskin belted with a wisp of bark. He ran free on the mesa and mountain where he would, and carried in his hand a cleft stick that had a longish rounded stone caught in the cleft and held by strips of skin. By this he knew he had waked up into the time of which the Basket Woman had told him, before fire was brought to the tribes, when men and beasts talked together with understanding, and the Coyote was the Friend and Counselor of man. They ranged together by wood and open swale, the boy who was to be called Fire Bringer and the keen, gray dog of the wilderness, and saw the tribesmen catching fish in the creeks with their hands and the women digging roots with sharp stones. This they did in summer and fared well, but when winter came they ran nakedly

55

in the snow or huddled in eaves of the rocks and were very miserable. When the boy saw this he was very unhappy, and brooded over it until the Coyote noticed it.

"It is because my people suffer and have no way to escape the cold," said the boy.

"I do not feel it," said the Coyote.

"That is because of your coat of good fur, which my people have not, except they take it in the chase, and it is hard to come by."

"Let them run about, then," said the Counselor, "and keep warm."

"They run till they are weary," said the boy, "and there are the young children and the very old. Is there no way for them?"

"Come," said the Coyote, "let us go to the hunt."

"I will hunt no more," the boy answered him, "until I have found a way to save my people from the cold. Help me, O Counselor!"

But the Coyote had run away. After a time he came back and found the boy still troubled in his mind.

"There is a way, O Man Friend," said the Coyote, "and you and I must take it together, but it is very hard."

"I will not fail of my part," said the boy.

"We will need a hundred men and women, strong and swift runners."

"I will find them," the boy insisted, "only tell me."

"We must go," said the Coyote, "to the Burning Mountain by the Big Water and bring fire to your people."

Said the boy, "What is fire?"

Then the Coyote considered a long time how he should tell the boy what fire is. "It is," said he, "red like a flower, yet it is no flower; neither is it a beast, though it runs in the grass and rages in the wood and devours all. It is very fierce and hurtful and stays not for asking, yet if it is kept among stones and fed with small sticks, it will serve the people well and keep them warm."

"How is it to be come at?"

"It has its lair in the Burning Mountain, and the Fire Spirits guard it night and day. It is a hundred days' journey from this place, and because of the jealousy of the Fire Spirits no man dare go near it. But I, because all beasts are known to fear it much, may approach it without hurt and, it may be, bring you a brand from the burning. Then you must have strong runners for every one of the hundred days to bring it safely home."

"I will go and get them," said the boy; but it was not so easily done as said. Many there were who were slothful and many were afraid, but the most disbelieved it wholly, for, they said, "How should this boy tell us of a thing of which we have never heard!" But at the last the boy and their own misery persuaded them.

The Coyote advised them how the march should begin. The boy and the Counselor went foremost, next to them the swiftest runners, with the others following in the order of their strength and speed. They left the place of their home and went over the high mountains where great jagged peaks stand up above the snow, and down the way the streams led through a long stretch of giant wood where the sombre shade and the sound of the wind in the branches made them afraid. At nightfall where they rested one stayed in that place, and the next night another dropped behind, and so it was at the end of each day's journey. They crossed a great plain where waters of mirage rolled over a cracked and parching earth and the rim of the world was hidden in a bluish mist; so they came at last to another range of hills, not so high but tumbled thickly together, and beyond these, at the end of the hundred days, to the Big Water quaking along the sand at the foot of the Burning Mountain.

It stood up in a high and peaked cone, and the smoke of its burning rolled out and broke along the sky. By night the glare of it reddened the waves far out on the Big Water when the Fire Spirits began their dance.

Then said the Counselor to the boy who was soon to be called the Fire Bringer, "Do you stay here until I bring you a brand from the burning; be ready and right for running, and lose no time, for I shall be far spent when I come again, and the Fire Spirits will pursue me." Then he went up the mountain, and the Fire Spirits when they saw him come were laughing and very merry, for his appearance was much against him. Lean he was, and his coat much the worse for the long way he had come. Slinking he looked, inconsiderable, scurvy, and mean, as he has always looked, and it served him as well then as it serves him now. So the Fire Spirits only laughed, and paid him no farther heed. Along in the night, when they came out to begin their dance about the mountain, the Coyote stole the fire and began to run away with it down the slope of the Burning Mountain. When the Fire Spirits saw what he had done, they streamed out after him red and angry in pursuit, with a sound like a swarm of bees.

The boy saw them come, and stood up in his place clean limbed and taut for running. He saw the sparks of the brand stream back along the Coyote's flanks as he carried it in his mouth and stretched forward on the trail, bright against the dark bulk of the mountain like a falling star. He heard the singing sound of the Fire Spirits behind and the labored breath of the Counselor nearing through the dark. Then the good beast panted down beside him, and the brand dropped from his jaws. The boy caught it up, standing bent for the running as a bow to speeding the arrow; out he shot on the homeward path, and the Fire Spirits snapped and sung behind him. Fast as they pursued he fled faster, until he saw the next runner stand up in his place to receive the brand. So it passed from hand to hand, and the Fire Spirits tore after it through the scrub until they came to the mountains of the snows. These they could not pass, and the dark, sleek runners with the backward-streaming brand bore it forward, shining star-like in the night, glowing red through sultry noons, violet pale in twilight glooms, until they came in safety to their own land. Here they kept it among stones, and fed it with small sticks, as the Coyote had advised, until it warmed them and cooked their food. As for the boy by whom fire came to the tribes, he was called the Fire Bringer while he lived, and after that, since there was no other with so good a right to the name, it fell to the Coyote; and this is the sign that the tale is true, for all along his lean flanks the fur is singed and yellow as it was by the flames that blew backward from the brand when he brought it down from the Burning Mountain. As for the fire, that went on broadening and brightening and giving out a cheery sound until it broadened into the light of day, and Alan sat up to hear it crackling under the coffee-pot, where his father was cooking their breakfast.

THE CROOKED FIR

The pipsissawa, which is sometimes called prince's pine, is half as tall as the woodchuck that lives under the brown boulder; and the seedling fir in his first season was as tall as the prince's pine, so for the time they made the most of each other's company. The woodchuck and the pipsissawa were never to be any taller, but the silver fir was to keep on growing as long as he stood in the earth and drew sap. In his second season, which happened to be a good growing year, the fir was as tall as the woodchuck and began to look about him.

The forest of silver firs grew on a hill-slope up from a watercourse as far as the borders of the long-leaved pines. Where the trees stood close together the earth was brown with the litter of a thousand years, and little gray hawks hunted in their green, windy glooms. In the open spaces there were thickets of meadowsweet, fireweed, monkshood, and columbine, with saplings and seedlings in between. When the fir which was as tall as the woodchuck had grown a year or two longer, he made a discovery. All the firs on the hill-slope were crooked! Their trunks bulged out at the base toward the downward pitch of the hill; and it is the proper destiny of fir trees to be straight.

"They should be straight," said the seedling fir. "I feel it in my fibres that a fir tree should be straight." He looked up at the fir mother very far above him on her way to the sky, with the sun and the wind in her star-built boughs.

"I shall be straight," said the seedling fir.

"Ah, do not be too sure of it," said the fir mother. But for all that the seedling fir was very sure, and when the snow tucked him in for the winter he took a long time to think about it. The snows are wonderfully deep in the cañon of the silver firs. From where they gather in the upper air the fir mother shakes them lightly down, packing so softly and so warm that the seedlings and the pipsissawas do not mind.

About the time the fir had grown tall enough to be called a sapling he made another discovery. The fir mother had also a crooked trunk. The sapling was greatly shocked; he hardly liked to speak of it to the fir mother. He remembered his old friend the pipsissawa, but he had so outgrown her that there was really no comfort in trying to make himself understood, so he spoke to the woodchuck. The woodchuck was no taller than he used to be, but when he climbed up on the brown boulder above his house he was on a level with the sapling fir, and though he was not much of a talker he was a great thinker and had opinions.

"Really," said the fir, "I hardly like to speak of it, but you are such an old friend; do you see what a crook the fir mother has in her trunk? We firs you know were intended to be straight."

"That," said the woodchuck, "is on account of the snow."

"But, oh, my friend," said the sapling, "you must be mistaken. The snow is soft and comfortable and braces one up. I ought to know, for I spend whole winters in it."

"*Gru—r—ru—,*" said the woodchuck crossly; "well for you that you do, or I should have eaten you off by now."

After this the little fir kept his thoughts to himself; he was very much afraid of the woodchuck, and there is nothing a young fir fears so much as being eaten off before it has a chance to bear cones. But in fact the woodchuck spent the winter under the snow himself. He went into his house and shut the door when the first feel of snow was in the air, and did not come out until green things began to grow in the cleared spaces.

Not many winters after that the fir was sufficiently tall to hold the green cross, that all firs bear on their topmost bough, above the snow most of the winter through. Now he began to learn a great many things. The first of these was about the woodchuck.

"Really that fellow is a great braggart," said the fir; "I cannot think how I came to be afraid of him."

In those days the sapling saw the deer getting down in the flurry of the first snows to the feeding grounds on the lower hills, saw the mountain sheep nodding their great horns serenely in the lee of a tall cliff through the wildest storms. In the spring he saw the brown bears shambling up the trails, ripping the bark off of dead trees to get at the worms and grubs that harbored there; lastly he saw the woodchuck come out of his hole as if nothing had ever happened.

And now as the winters came on, the fir began to feel the weight of the snow. When it was wet and heavy and clung to its branches, the little fir shivered and moaned.

"Droop your boughs," creaked the fir mother; "droop them as I do, and the snow will fall."

So the sapling drooped his fan-spread branches until they lay close to the trunk; and the snow wreaths slipped away and piled thickly about his trunk. But when the snow lay deep over all the slope, it packed and slid down toward the ravine and pressed strongly against the sapling fir.

"Oh, I shall be torn from my roots," he cried; "I shall be broken off."

"Bend," said the fir mother, "bend, and you will not break." So the young fir bent before the snow until he was curved like a bow, but when the spring came and the sap ran in his veins, he straightened his trunk anew and spread his branches in a star-shaped whorl.

"After all," said the sapling, "it is not such a great matter to keep straight; it only requires an effort."

So he went on drooping and bending to the winter snows, growing strong and straight with the spring, and rejoicing. About this time the fir began to feel a tingling in his upper branches.

"Something is going to happen," he said; something agreeable in fact, for the tree was fifty years old, and it was time to grow cones. For fifty years a silver fir has nothing to do but to grow branches, thrown out in annual circles, every one in the shape of a cross. Then it grows cones on the topmost whorl, royal purple and burnished gold, erect on the ends of the branches like Christmas candles. The sapling fir had only three in his first season of bearing, but he was very proud of them, for now he was no longer a sapling, but a tree.

When one has to devote the whole of a long season to growing cones, one has not much occasion to think of other things. By the time there were five rows of cone-bearing branches spread out broadly from the silver fir, the woodchuck made a remark to the pipsissawa which is sometimes called prince's pine. It was not the same pipsissawa, nor the same woodchuck, but one of his descendants, and his parents had told him the whole story.

"It seems to me," said he, "that the fir tree is not going to be straight after all. He never seems quite to recover from the winter snow."

"Ah," said the pipsissawa, "I have always thought it better to have your seeds ripe and put away under ground before the snow comes. Then you do not mind it at all."

The woodchuck was right about the fir; his trunk was beginning to curve toward the downward slope of the hill with the weight of the drifts. And that went on until the curve was quite fixed in the ripened wood, and the fir tree could not have straightened up if he had wished. But to tell the truth, the fir tree did not wish. By the end of another fifty years, when he wagged his high top above the forest gloom, he grew to be quite proud of it.

"There is nothing," he said to the sapling firs, "like being able to endure hard times with a good countenance. I have seen a great deal of life. There are no such snows now as there used to be. You can see by the curve of my trunk what a weight I have borne."

But the young firs did not pay any attention to him. They had made up their minds to grow up straight.

THE SUGAR PINE

Before the sugar pine came up in the meadow of Bright Water it had swung a summer long in the burnished cone of the parent tree, until the wind lifted it softly to the earth where it swelled with the snow water and the sun, and began to grow into a tree. But it knew nothing whatever of itself except that it was alive and growing; and in its first season was hardly so tall as the Little Grass of Parnassus that crowded the sod at the Bright Water. In fact, it was a number of years before it began to overtop the meadowsweet, the fireweed, the tall lilies, the monkshood, and columbine, and under these circumstances it could not be expected to have much of an opinion of itself.

During those years the young pine suffered a secret mortification because it had no flowers. It stood stiff and trimly in its plain dark green, every needle like every other one, and no honey-gatherer visited it. When all the meadow ran over with rosy and purple bloom, the pine tree trembled and beads of clear resin oozed out upon its bark like tears; and the trouble really seemed worse than it was because everybody made so much of it. Even the hummingbirds as they came hurtling through the air would draw back conspicuously when they came to the pine, and though they said politely, "I beg your pardon, I took you for a flower," the seedling felt it would have been better had they said nothing at all.

"Well, why don't you grow flowers?" said the meadowsweet; "it is easy enough. Just do as I do," and she spread her drift of blossoms like a fragrant snow. But the sugar pine found it impossible to be anything but stiff and plainly green, though every year in the stir and tingle of new sap he felt a promise of better things.

"I suppose," he said one day, "I must be in some way different from the rest of you."

"Ah, that is the way with you solemn people," said the fireweed, "always imagining yourself better than those about you to excuse your disagreeableness. Any one can see by the way you hold yourself that you have too much of an opinion of yourself."

The little pine tree sighed; he had not said "better," only "different," and he began to realize year by year that this was so.

"You should try to be natural," said the meadowsweet; "do not be so stiff, and then every one will love you though you are so plain."

Then the sugar pine reached out and tried to mingle with the flowers, but the sharp needles tore their frills and the stiff branches did not suit with their graceful swaying, so he was obliged to give it up. It seemed, in fact, the more he tried to be like the others the worse he grew.

"If only you were not so odd," said all the flowers. None of the young growing things in the meadow understood that it is natural for a pine tree to be stiff.

The sugar pine was not always unhappy. There were days when he caught golden glints of the stream that ran smoothly about the meadow, in a bed of leopard-colored stones, and, reflecting all the light that fell into the hollow of the hills, gave the place its name; days when the air was warm and the sky was purely blue, and the resinous smell of the pines on the meadow border came to the seedling like a sweet savor in a dream, for as yet he did not understand what he was to be. He was pleased just to be looking at the summer riot of the flowering things, and loved the cool softness of the snow when he was tucked into comfortable darkness to dream of the spring odor of the pines. Then, when it seemed that the meadow had forgotten him, the little tree would fall to thinking the thoughts proper to his kind, and found the time pass pleasantly.

"I suppose," he thought, "it is not good for me to flower as the other plants. If I began like them I should probably end like them and I feel that I could not be satisfied with that. After all, one should not try to be so much like others, but to be the very best of one's own sort."

Very early the young tree had noticed that he was the only one of all that company that kept green and growing the winter through. He would have been secretly very proud of it, but the flowers took good care to let him know their opinion of such airs.

"It is simply that you wish to be considered peculiar," said the columbine; "one sees that you like nothing so much as to be in other people's mouths, but let me tell you, you will not get yourself any better liked by such behavior." After that the little tree wished nothing so much as that he might be the commonest summer-flowering weed.

"But I am not," he said; "no, I am not, and I would do very well as I am if they would let me be happy in my own way."

That summer the seedling grew as tall as the meadowsweet, and could look across the open space to the parent pine poised on her noble shaft, her spreading crown gathering sunshine from the draughts of upper air. She seemed to rock a little as if she dozed upon her feet, and the great sweep of limbs with pendulous golden cones made a gentle sighing. Then the despised little seedling felt a thrill go through him, and felt a shaking in all his slender twigs. He bowed himself among the lilies, and was both glad and ashamed, for though he could not well believe it, he knew himself akin to the great sugar pines. After that he gave up trying to be one of the flowers. Once he even ventured to speak of it to the meadowsweet.

"Well, if it is any satisfaction to you to think so; but do not let any one else hear you say that. You are likely to get yourself misunderstood. I tell you this because I am your friend," said the meadowsweet, but really she had misunderstood him herself.

Then a rumor arose in the neighborhood that the sombre, stubborn shrub conceited himself to be a pine, and the rumor ran with laughter and nodding the length of the meadow until it reached the old alder on the edge of Bright Water. The alder had stood with his feet in the stream for longer than the meadowsweet could remember, and saw everything that went on by reflection.

"Do not laugh too soon," said the alder tree, "I have seen stranger things than that happen in this meadow," for he was indeed very old.

"We have known him a good many seasons," said the fireweed, "and he has not done anything worth mentioning yet."

All this was very hard for the young pine to bear, but there was better coming. That summer the forest ranger came riding in Bright Water and a learned man rode with him, praising the flowers and counting the numbers and varieties of bloom. How they prinked and flaunted in their pride!

"That is all very pretty, as you say," answered the ranger as they came by the place of the pine, "and I suppose they perform a sort of service in keeping the soil covered, but the trees are the real strength of the mountain. Ah, here is a seedling of the right sort! I must give that fellow a chance, and he began pulling up great handfuls of the blossoming things around the tree.

"What is it?" asked his companion.

"A sugar pine," he said; "probably a seedling of that splendid specimen yonder," and he went on clearing the ground to let in sun and air.

"But you must admit," said his friend, "that a seedling pine cuts rather a poor figure among all this flare of bloom."

"Oh, you wait fifty or sixty years," said the ranger, "and then you will see what sort of a figure it makes. It really takes a pine of this sort a couple of hundred years to reach its prime," and they rode talking up the trail.

Word of what had happened was carried all about the meadow and made a great stir. When it came to the alder tree he wagged his old head. "Ah, well," he said, "I told you so."

"I will not believe it until I see it," said the fireweed. "They might have known it before," sighed the young pine, "and they ought to be proud to think I grew up in the same meadow with them."

But they were not; they went on flaunting their blossoms as if nothing had occurred, and the young tree grew up as he was meant to be, and the pines on the meadow border sent him greeting on the wind. He still kept his trim spire-shaped habit, but he could very well put up with that for the time being. He felt within himself the promise of what he was to be. After fifty or sixty years, as the ranger had said, he began to put out strong cone-bearing boughs that shaped themselves by the storms and the wind in sweeping, graceful lines, and spread out to shelter the horde of flowering things below. Squirrels ran up the trunk and whistled cheerily in his windy top.

"He grew here in our neighborhood," said the tall lilies; "we knew him when he was a seedling sprig, and now he is the tallest of the pines."

"Suppose he is," said the fireweed. "What is the good of a pine tree anyway?"

But the sugar pine did not hear. He had grown far above the small folk of the meadow, and went on growing for a hundred years. He gathered the sun in his high branches and rocked upon his shaft. He talked gently in his own fashion with his own kind.

THE GOLDEN FORTUNE

A little way up from the trail that goes toward Rex Monte, not far from the limit of deep snows, there is what looks to be a round dark hole in the side of the mountain. It is really the ruined tunnel of an old mine. Formerly a house stood on the ore dump at one side of the tunnel, a little unpainted cabin of pine; but a great avalanche of snow and stones carried them, both the house and the dump, away. The cabin was built and owned by a solitary miner called Jerry, and whether he ever had any other name no one in the town below Kearsarge now remembers.

Jerry was old and lean, and his hair, which had been dark when he was young, was now bleached to the color of the iron-rusted rocks about his mine. For thirty years he had prospected and mined through that country from Kearsarge to the Coso Hills, but always in the pay of other men, and at last he had hit upon this ledge on Rex Monte. To all who looked, it showed a very slender vein between the walls of country rock, and the ore of so poor a quality that with all his labor he could do no more than keep alive; but to all who listened, Jerry could tell a remarkable story of what it had been, and what he expected it to be. Very many years ago he had discovered it at the end of a long prospect, when he was tired and quite discouraged for that time. There was not much passing then on the Rex Monte, and Jerry drew out of the trail here in the middle of the afternoon to rest in the shadow of a great rock. So while he lay there very weary, between sleeping and waking, he gazed out along the ground, which was all strewn with rubble between the stiff, scant grass. As he looked it seemed that certain bits of broken stone picked themselves out of the heap, and grew larger, in some way more conspicuous, until, Jerry averred, they winked at him. Then he reached out to draw them in with his hand, and saw that they were all besprinkled with threads and specks of gold. You may guess that Jerry was glad, then that he sprang up and began to search for more stones, and so found a trail of them, and followed it through the grass stems and the heather until he came to the ledge cropping out by a dike of weathered rocks. And in those days the ledge was ah, so rich! Now it seemed that Jerry was to have a mine of his own. So he named it the Golden Fortune, and told no man what he had found, but went down to the town which lies in a swale at the foot of Kearsarge, and brought back as much as was needful for working the mine in a simple way.

It was nearing the end of the summer, when the hills expect the long thunder and drumming rain, and, not many weeks after that, the quiet storms that bring the snow. Jerry had enough to do to make all safe and comfortable at the Golden Fortune before winter set in. It was too steep here on the hill-slope for the deep snows to trouble him much, so he built his cabin against the rock, with a covered way from it to the tunnel of the mine, that he might work on all winter at no unease because of storms.

It was perhaps a month later, with Jerry as busy as any of the wild folk thereabout, and the nights turning off bitter cold with frost. Of mornings he could hear the thin tinkle of the streams along fringes of delicate ice. It was the afternoon of a day that fell warm and dry with a promise of snow in the air. Jerry was roofing in his cabin, so intent that a voice hailed him before he was aware that there was a man on the trail. Jerry knew at once by his dress and his speech that he was a stranger in those parts, and he saw that he was not very well prepared for the mountain passes and the night. He knew this, I say, with the back of his mind, but took no note of it, for he was so occupied with his house and his mine. He suffered a fear to have any man know of his good fortune lest it should somehow slip away from him. So when the stranger asked him some questions of the trail, it seemed that what Jerry most wished was to get rid of him as quickly as possible. He was a young man, ruddy and blue-eyed, and a foreigner, what was called in careless miners' talk, "some kind of a Dutchman," and could not make himself well understood. Jerry gathered that he desired to know if he were headed right for the trail that went over to the Bighorn Mine, where he had the promise of work. So they nodded and shrugged, and Jerry made assurance with his hands, as much as to say, it is no great way; and when the young man had looked wistfully at the cabin and the boding sky, he moved slowly up the trail. When he came to the turn where it goes toward Rex Monte, he lingered on the ridge to wave good-by, so Jerry waved again, and the man dropped out of sight. At that moment the sun failed behind a long gray film that deepened and spread over all that quarter of the sky.

Jerry had cause to remember the stranger in the night and fret for him, for the wind came up and began to seek in the cañon, and the snow fell slanting down. It fell three days and nights. All that while the gray veil hung about Jerry's house; now and then the wind would scoop a great lane in it to show how the drifts lay on the heather, then shut in tight and dim with a soft, weary sound, and Jerry, though he worked on the Golden Fortune, could not get the young stranger out of his mind.

When the sun and the frost had made a crust over the snow able to bear up a man, he went over the Pass to Bighorn to inquire if the stranger had come in, though he did not tell at that time, nor until long after, how late it was when the man passed his cabin, how wistfully he turned away, nor what promise was in the air. The snow lay all about the Pass, lightly on the pines, deeply in the hollows, so deeply that a man might lie under it and no one be the wiser. And there it seemed the stranger must be, for at the Bighorn they had not heard of him, but if he were under the snow, there he must lie until the spring thaw. Of whatever happened to him, Jerry saw that he must bear the blame, for, by his own account, from that day the luck vanished from the Golden Fortune; not that the ore dwindled or grew less, but there were no more of the golden specks. With all he could do after that, Jerry could not maintain himself in the cabin on the slope of Rex Monte. So it came about that the door was often shut, and the picks rusted in the tunnel of the Golden Fortune for months together, while Jerry was off earning wages in more prosperous mines.

All his days Jerry could not quite get his mind away from the earlier promise of the mine, and as often as he thought of that he thought of the stranger whom he had sent over the trail on the evening of the storm. Gradually it came into his mind in a confused way that the two things were mysteriously connected, that he had sent away his luck with the stranger into the deep snow. For certainly Jerry held himself accountable, and in that country between Kearsarge and the Coso Hills to be inhospitable is the worst offense.

Every year or so he came back to the mine to work a little, and sometimes it seemed to promise better and sometimes not. Finally, Jerry argued that the luck would not come back to it until he had made good to some other man the damage he had done to one. This set him looking for an opportunity. Jerry mentioned his belief so often that he came at last, as is the way of miners, to accept it as a thing prophesied of old time. Afterward, when he grew old himself, and came to live out his life at the Golden Fortune, he would be always looking along the trail at evening time for passers-by, and never one was allowed to go on who could by any possibility be persuaded to stay the night in Jerry's cabin. Often when there was a wind, and the snow came slanting down, Jerry fancied he heard one shouting in the drift; then he would light a lantern and sally forth into the storm, peering and crying.

About that time, when he went down into the town below Kearsarge once in a month or so for supplies, the people smiled and wagged their heads, but Jerry conceived that they whispered together about the unkindness he had done to the stranger so many years gone, and he grew shyer and went less often among men. So he companioned more with the wild things, and burrowed deeper into the hill. His cabin weathered to a semblance of the stones, rabbits ran in and out at the door, and deer drank at his spring.

From the slope where the cabin stood, the trail, which led up from the town, winding with the winding of the cañon, went over the Pass, and so into a region of high meadows and high, keen peaks, the feeding-ground of deer and mountain sheep. The ravine of Rex Monte was the easiest going from the high valleys to the foothills, where all winter the feed kept green. Every year Jerry marked the trooping of the wild kindred to the foothill pastures when the snow lay heavily on all the higher land, and saw their returning when the spring pressed hard upon the borders of the melting drifts. So, as he grew older and stayed closer by his mine, Jerry learned to look to the furred and feathered folk for news of how the seasons fared, and what was doing on the high ridges. When the grouse and quail went down, it was a sign that the snow had covered the grass and small seed-bearing herbs; the passing of deer—shapely bulks in a mist of cloud—was a portent of deep drifts over the buckthorn and the heather. Lastly, if he saw the light fleeting of the mountain sheep, he looked for wild and bitter work on the crest of Kearsarge and Rex Monte. It was mostly at such times that Jerry heard voices in the storm, and he would go stumbling about with his lantern into the swirl of falling snow, until the wind that played up and down the great cañon, like the draughts in a chimney, made his very bones a-cold. Then he would creep back to drowse by the warmth of his fire and dream that the blue-eyed stranger had come back and brought the luck of the Golden Fortune. So he passed the years until the winter of the Big Snow. It was so called many winters after, for no other like it ever fell on the east slope of Kearsarge.

It came early in the season, following a week of warm weather, when the sky was full of a dry mist that showed ghostly gray against the sun and the moon; great bodies of temperate air moved about the pines with a sound of moaning and distress. The deer, warned by their wild sense, went down before ever a flake fell, and Jerry, watching, shivered in sympathy, recalling that so they had run together, and such a spell of warm weather had gone before a certain snow, years ago before the luck departed from the Golden Fortune. As the fume of the storm closed in about the cabin, and flakes began to form lightly in the middle air, the old man's wits began to fumble among remembrances of the stranger on the trail, and he would hearken for voices. The snow began, then increased, and fell steadily, wet and blinding.

The third night of its falling Jerry waked out of a doze to hear his name shouted, muffled and feebly, through the drift. So it seemed to him, and he made haste to answer it. There was no wind; on the very steep slope where the cabin stood was a knee-deep level, soft and clogging; in the hollows it piled halfway up the pines. Jerry's lantern threw a faint and stifled gleam. There was no further cry, but something struggled on the trail below him; dim, unhuman shapes wrestled in the smother of the snow. Jerry sent them a hail of assurance cut off short by the white wall of the storm.

There was a little sag in the hill-front where the trail turned off to the cabin, and here the moist snow fell in a lake, into which the trail ran like a spit, and was lost. Down this trail at the last fierce end of the storm came the great wild sheep, the bighorn, the heaviest-headed, lightest-footed, winter-proof sheep of the mountains that God shepherds on the high battlements of the hills. Down they came when there was no meadow, nor thicket, nor any smallest twig of heather left uncovered on the highlands, and took the lake of soggy snow by Jerry's cabin in the dark. They had come far under the weight of the great curved horns through the clogging drifts. Here where the trail failed in the white smudge they found no footing, floundered at large,

sinking belly-deep where they stood, and not daring to stand
lest they sink deeper. If any cry of theirs, hoarse and broken, had
reached old Jerry's dreaming, they spent no further breath on it.
By something the same sense that made him aware of their need,
Jerry understood rather than saw them strain through the falling veil of snow. It was a sharp struggle without sound as they
won out of the wet drift to the firmer ground. They went on like
shadows pursued by the ghost of a light that wavered with the
old man's wavering feet. It was no night for a man to be abroad
in, but Jerry plowed on in the drift till he found the work that
was cut out for him. There where the snow was deepest, yielding
like wool, he found the oldest wether of the flock, sunk to the
shoulders, too feeble for the struggle, and still too noble for complaining. How many years had Jerry waited to do a good turn on
the trail where he had done his worst: and in all these years he
had lost the sense of distinction which should be between man
and beast. He put his shoulder under the fore shoulder of the
sheep, where he could feel the heart pound with certain fear.

Jerry knew the trail, as he knew the floor of his mine, by the
feel of the ground under him, so as he heaved and guided with
his shoulder, the great ram grew quieter and lent himself to the
effort till they came clear of the swale and the sweat ran down
from Jerry's forehead. But the bighorn could do no more. In the
soft fleece of the snow he stood cowed and trembling. The snow
came on faster, and wiped out the trail of the flock; he made no
motion to go after. Such a death comes to the wild sheep of the
mountains often enough: to fail from old age in some sudden
storm, to sink in the loose snow and await the quest of the wolf,
or the colder mercy of the drift. He turned his back to the storm
which began to slant a little with the rising wind, and looked not

once at Jerry nor at the hills where he had been bred. But Jerry cast his eye upon the sheep, which was full heavier then than he, and then up at the steep where his cabin stood, remembering that he had nothing there that might serve a sheep for food. Then he bent down again, and by dint of pulling and pushing, and by a dim sense that began to filter through the man's brain to the beast, they made some progress on the trail. They went over broken boulders and floundered in the drifts, where Jerry half carried the sheep and was half borne up and supported by the spread of the great horns. They crossed Pine Creek, which ran dumbly under the snow, housed over by the stream tangle. The flakes hissed softly on Jerry's lantern and struck blindingly on his eyes, but ever as they went the sheep was eased of his labor, grew assured, and carried himself courageously. Finally they came where the storm thinned out, and whole hill-slopes covered with buckthorn and cherry warded off the snow by springy arches, and Jerry drew up to rest under a long-leaved pine while the sheep went on alone, nodding his great horns under the branches of the scrub. He neither lingered nor looked back, and met the new chance of life with as much quietness as the chance of death. Jerry was worn and weary, and there was a singing in his brain. The pine trees broke the wind and shed off the snow in curling wreaths. It seemed to the old man most good to rest, and he drowsed upon his feet.

"If I sleep I shall freeze," he said; and it seemed on the whole a pleasant thing to do. So it went on for a little space; then there came a shape out of the dark, a hand shook him by the shoulder, and a voice called him by name. Then he started out of dreaming as he had started at that other call an hour ago, and it seemed not strange to him, the night, nor the storm, nor the face of the blue-eyed man that shone out of the dark, but whether by the light of his lantern he could not tell. He shook the snow from his shoulders.

"I have expected you long," he said.

"And now I have come," said the stranger and smiled.

"Have you brought the luck again?"

"Come and see," said the man.

Then Jerry took his hand and leaned upon him, and together they went up the trail between the drifts.

"You bear me no ill-will for what I did?" said Jerry.

And the stranger answered, "None."

"I have wished it undone many times," said the old man. "I have tried this night to repay it."

"By what you have done this night I am repaid," said the stranger.

"It was only a sheep."

"It was one of God's creatures," said the man.

So they went on up the trail, and it seemed sometimes to Jerry that he wandered alone in the dark, that he was cold, and his lantern had gone out; and again he would hear the stranger comfort him and encourage him. At last they came toward the cabin, and saw the light stream out of the window and the fire leap in the stove. Then Jerry thought of the mine, and that the stranger had brought back the luck again. It seemed that the young man had promised him this, though he could not be sure of that, nor very clear in his mind on any point except that he had come home again. But as he drew near, it seemed a brightness came out of the tunnel of the mine, a warmth and a great light. As he came into it tremblingly, he saw that the light came from the walls, and from the lode at the far end of it, and it was the brightness of pure gold. And Jerry smiled and stretched out his arms to it, making sure that the luck had come again.

After the week of the Big Snow there were people in the town who remembered Jerry, and wondered how he fared. So when the snow had a crust over it, they came up by the windy cañon and sought him in his house, where the door stood open and a charred wick flared feebly in the lamp, and in his mine, where they found him at the far end of the tunnel, and it seemed as if he slept and smiled.

"It is a worthless lode," they said, "but he loved it."

So they took powder and made a blast, and with it a great heap of stones, shutting off the end of the tunnel from the outer air, and so left him with his luck and the Golden Fortune.

THE WHITE-BARKED PINE

The white-barked pine grew on the slope of Kearsarge highest up of all the pines, so high that nothing grew above it but brown tufts of grass and the rosy Sierra primroses that shelter under the edges of broken boulders. The white-barked pines are squat and short, trunks creeping along the rocks, and foliage all matted in a close green thatch by the winter's weight. Snow lies on the slope of Kearsarge eight months in the year, deep and smooth over the pines and the jagged rocks; other months there are great storms of rain, and always a strong wind roaring through the Pass, so that, try as it might, no tree could stand erect on those heights. The white-barked pine stretched its body along the ground, and though it was four hundred years old, it was no thicker than a man's leg, and its young branches of seventy-five or a hundred years were still so supple that one could tie knots in them. It grew near the trail, which here crossed through a gap in the crest of the range and straggled on down the other side of the mountain.

Along this trail went many strange things in their season. Early in the year, before the snow had melted at all on the high places, went a great lumbering bear that had a lair above Big Meadows, going down to the calf-pens and pig-sties of the town at the foot of Kearsarge. He ranged back and forth on these little excursions of fifteen or twenty miles in the hungry season of the year, and sometimes there were hunters on his trail with dogs and guns, but nothing ever came of it. When the trail began to run a rivulet from the drip of melting snow banks, the forest ranger went up the Pass, singing as he went and beating his arms to keep himself warm. Afterwards when the snow water was all drained off, he came back and mended the trail. All through the summer there would be parties of miners and hunters with long strings of pack mules, going over Kearsarge to camp in Big Meadows or on the fork of King's River. Sometimes there were parties of Indians with women and children, making very merry with berries, fish, and deer meat. Nearly always, whatever went over the mountain came back again, and the white pine noticed that the same people came again another season. In four hundred years one has space for observation and reflection. Gradually the pine tree grew into the conviction that the other side of the mountain must be much finer than this.

"Else why," said he, "should so many people go there every year?"

It was very fine, you may be sure, on the white pine's side, but the tree had known it all for so many years, it no longer pleased him. From where he grew he looked down between the ridges on a great winding cañon full of singing trees, with blue lakes like eyes winking between them. He could watch in the open places the white feet of the water on its way to the valley, and from the falls long rainbows of spray blown out as if they were blowing kisses to the white-barked pine. Below all this lay the valley, hollow like a cup, full of fawn-colored and violet mist, and the farms and orchards lay like dregs at the bottom of the cup. Beyond the valley rose other noble ranges with cloud shadows playing all along their slopes.

83

"It is very tiresome to look at the same things for four hundred years," said the white-barked pine. "If I could only get to the top, now. Do tell me, what is it like on the other side?" he said to the wind.

"Oh!" said the wind, "it rains and snows. There are trees and bushes and blue lakes. It is not at all different from this side."

A deer said the same thing when it slept one night under the thatch of the highest pine. "It is all meadows and hills, only sometimes the grass is not so good there, and again sometimes it is better. It is very much like this."

"I do not believe them," said the pine to himself. "They are simply trying to console me for not realizing my ambition. But I am not a sapling any longer, let me tell you that."

"At least," said a young tree that grew a little farther down, "you are higher up than any of us."

"Of what use is that if I do not get to the top?" said the unhappy pine. "There is a bunch of blue flowers there, I can see it quite plainly just where the trail dips over the ridge. Surely I am as capable of climbing as any blue weed."

"But," said the young pine, "weeds do not have to grow cones."

"Oh, as for cones," cried the tree quite crossly, "the seasons are so short I hardly ever ripen any, and if I do the squirrels get them. I do believe I have not started a seedling these two hundred years. It is no use to talk to me, I shall be happy only when I have seen the other side of the mountain."

It seems what one desires with all one's heart for a long time finally comes to pass in some fashion or other. That very season the white-barked pine went up over Kearsarge to the other side. Early in the summer, when the rosy primroses had just begun to blow beside the drifts that hugged the shade of the boulders, a party of miners went up the trail with a long string of pack mules burdened with picks and shovels, flour and potatoes, and other things that miners use. The last pull up the Kearsarge trail is the hardest, over a steep waste of loose stones that want very little encouragement to go roaring down as an avalanche into the ravine below. The miners shouted, the mules scrambled and panted on the steep, but just as they came by the last of the white-barked pines, one slipped and went rolling over and over on the jagged stones. As happens very frequently when a pack animal falls, the mule was not very much hurt, but the pack saddle was quite ruined.

"We must do the best we can," said one of the men, and he cut down the white-barked pine. He chopped off the boughs, and split the trunk in four pieces to mend the pack. It was a very small tree though it was so old.

"Ah! Ah!" said the tree, "it hurts, but one does not mind that when one is realizing an ambition. Now I shall go to the top." So he went over Kearsarge on mule-back quite like an old traveler.

"Well, we are rid of his complaining," said the pine who stood next to him, "and now I am the highest up of all the pines. I wonder if it is really so much finer on the other side."

His old companion, in four pieces, was swinging down the other side of the mountain, and as he went, he saw high peaks and soddy meadows, long winding cañons with white glancing waters; and heard the chorus of the falls. When it was night the miners lit a fire and loosened up the packs, and after dark, when the wind began to move among the trees and the fire burned low, one of the men threw a piece of the white-barked pine on it.

"Oh! Oh!" cried the pine as the flames caught hold of it, "and is this really the end of all my travels?"

"How that green wood sputters!" said the man; "it is not fit even for firewood."

The next day the wind took up the ash and carried it back over the pass, and dropped it where the chopped boughs lay fainting on the ground.

"Ah, is that you?" they said; "now you can tell us what it is like on the other side."

"How ignorant you are," said the ash of the white-barked pine, "one would know you have never traveled. It is exactly like this side." But he could not hear what they had to say to that, for the wind whirled him away.

NA'ŸANG-WIT'E,

THE FIRST RABBIT DRIVE

The Basket Woman was walking over the mesa with the great
carrier at her back. Behind her straggled the children and the
other women of the campoodie, each with a cone-shaped basket slung between her shoulders. Alan clapped his hands when
he saw them coming, and ran out along the path.

"You come see rabbit drive," she said, twinkling her shrewd
black eyes under the border of her basket cap. Alan took hold of
a fold of her dress as he walked beside her, for he was still a little
afraid of the other Indians, but since the time of his going out to
see the buzzards making a merry-go-round, he knew he should
never be afraid of the Basket Woman again. The other women
laughed a great deal as they looked at him, showing their white
teeth and putting back the black coarse hair out of their eyes,
and Alan felt that the things they said to each other were about
him, though they could hardly have been unpleasant with so
much smiling. Now he could see the men swarm out of the
huts under the hill, all afoot but a dozen of the old men, who
rode small kicking ponies at a tremendous pace, digging their
heels into the horses' ribs. They passed up the mesa in a blur
of golden dust; westward they dwindled to a speck, something
ran between them from man to man, now thick like a cord, then
shaken out and vanishing in air. Then the riders dropped from

their horses and fumbled on the ground. Alan plucked at the Basket Woman's dress.

"Tell me what it is they do," he said.

"It is the net which they set with forked stakes of willow," answered the Basket Woman. Now the young men and the middle-aged began to form a line across the mesa, standing three man's lengths apart in the sage. Some of them were armed with guns and others had only clubs; all were merry, laughing and calling to one another. They began to move forward evenly with a marching movement, beating the brush as they went. Presently up popped a rabbit from the sage and ran before them in long flying leaps; far down the line another bounded from a stony wash, his lean flanks turned broadside to the sun.

Then the hunters broke into shouts of laughter and clapping, then one began to sing and the song passed from man to man along the line; then the men crouched a little as Indians do in singing, then their bodies swayed and they stamped with each staccato note as they moved forward. Rabbits sprang up in the scrub and went before them like the wind, and as each one leaped into view and laid back his ears in flight, the cries and laughter grew and the singing rose louder. The wind blew it back to the women and children straggling far behind, who took it up, and the burden of it was this,—

E - ya - ha hi,   E - ya,   E - ya - hi!

But every man sang it for himself, beginning when he liked and leaving off, and when a rabbit started up under foot or one overleaped himself and went sprawling to the sand the refrain broke out again, but the words, when there were any, seemed not to have anything to do with the hunt, and sounded to Alan like a game.

"*He-yah-hi, hi!* he has it, he has it, he has the white, he has it!"

"*Na'ÿang-wit'e!* chuckled the Basket Woman. "*Na'ÿang-wit'e! na'ÿang-wit'e!*" It is as it was of old time, look now and you shall see."

Alan looked at the hunters again, and whether it was because of the blown dust of the mesa, or the quiver of heat that rose up from the sand, or because the Basket Woman had laid her hand upon him, he saw that they were not as they had been a moment since. Now they wore no hats and were naked from the waist up, clothed below with deerskin garments. Quivers of the skin of cougars with the tails hanging down were slung between their shoulders, and the arrows in them were pointed with tips of obsidian and winged with eagle feathers. Every man carried his bow or his spear in his hand. Bright beads and bits of many-colored shell hung and glittered in their hair. Rabbits went before them like grasshoppers for number, and the song and the shouting were fierce and wild. "But what is it all about?" asked Alan.

"*Na'ÿang-wit'e, na'ÿang-wit'e,*" laughed the Basket Woman. "Wait and I will tell you the story of that song, for it is so that every song has its story, without which no one may understand it. It is not well to go too near the guns; sit you here and I will tell."

So Alan bent down the sagebrush to make him a springy seat and the Basket Woman sat upon the ground with her hands clasped about her knees.

"Long and long ago," said the Basket Woman, "when men and

beasts talked together, there were none so friendly and none so much about the wickiups as the rabbit people, and some of our fathers have told that it was they who taught my people the game of *na'ÿang-wit'e*. I know not if that be true, but there were none so cunning as they to play it. And this is the manner of the game: there should be two sticks, or better, two bits of bone of the fore leg of a deer, made smooth and small to fit the palm. One of them is all white and the other has sinew of deer stained black and wound about it. These the players pass from hand to hand, and another will guess where is the place of the white, and he who guesses best shall win all the other's goods. It is good sport playing, and between man and man it comes even in the end, for sometimes one has the goods and sometimes another, but when my people played with the rabbit people it was not good, for the rabbits won every time. Then my people drew together, all the Indians of every sort, and made a great game against the rabbit people. There were two long rows across the mesa, and between them were all the goods piled high, all the beads and ornaments of shell, all the feather work and fine dressed deerskin, all the worked moccasins, the quivers, the bows, all the blankets, the baskets, and the woven mats. So they played at sunrise, so at noon, so when it was night and the fires were lit. So on into the night, and when it was morning the game was done, for the Indians had no more goods. "*Ay-aiy!*" said the Basket Woman, "long will the rabbit people sorrow for that day, for it was then that the Indians first contrived together how they might be rid of them. Then they gathered up the milkweed," and she reached out and plucked a tall stem of it growing beside her, white flowered and slender, with fine leaves like grass. "Then they broke it so," and she laid it across a stone and beat it lightly with a stick, "then they drew out the threads soft and white, and so they rolled it into string."

She stretched the fibre with one hand and rolled it on her knee with the other, twisting and twining it. "Thus was the string made and afterward woven into nets. The mesh of the net was just enough to let a rabbit's head through, but not his body, and the net was a little wider than a rabbit's jump when he goes fast and fleeing, and long enough to stretch half across the world. So on a day the net was set and the drive was begun as you have seen it, and as the Indians went they remembered their anger and taunted the rabbit people. So the song of *Na'ÿang-wit'e* was made. Now let us go and see how it fares with the rabbit people, for as it was of old so will it be to-day."

All this time the line of men moved steadily across the mesa toward the net. Now and then a rabbit turned, made bold by fright, and passed between the men as they marched. Then the nearest turned to shoot him as he ran, but it was left to the women to pick up the game. Already the foremost rabbits were at the net, turned back by it, leaping toward the hunters and fleeing again to the net. The old men closed in the ends of the lane where the rabbits ran about distractedly with shrill squeals of anguished fear. Some got their heads through the mesh but never their bodies, and as it is not the nature of rabbits to go backward they struggled and cried, getting themselves the more entangled; some blind with their haste came against it in mid-leap, and were thrown back stunned upon the sand. The men sang no more, for they had work to do, serious work, for on the dried flesh of the rabbits and the blankets made of their skins the campoodie must largely count for food and warmth in the win-ter season. They closed in to the killing and made short work of it with clubs and the butt ends of their guns. Then the women came up with the children and heaped up the great carriers with the game while the men wrung the sweat from their foreheads and counted up the kill. Most of the rabbits were the kind Alan had learned to call jack rabbits, but the Basket Woman picked up a fat little cotton-tail.

"This is little Tavwots," said she, "and you shall have him for your supper." Alan's mind still ran on the story of the first drive. "But is it true?" he asked her, before he had given thanks for the gift.

"Now this is the sign I shall give you that the tale is true," said the Basket Woman. "Ever since that day if one of the rabbit people meets an Indian in the trail he flees before him as you saw them flee to-day, and that is because of *na'ÿang-wit'e* and the first rabbit drive." Then she laughed, but Alan took his share of the kill on his shoulder and went back across the mesa slowly, wondering.

MAHALA JOE

In the campoodie of Three Pines, which you probably know better by its Spanish name of Tres Pinos, there is an Indian, well thought of among his own people, who goes about wearing a woman's dress, and is known as Mahala Joe. He should be about fifty years old by this time, and has a quiet, kindly face. Sometimes he tucks up the skirt of his woman's dress over a pair of blue overalls when he has a man's work to do, but at feasts and dances he wears a ribbon around his waist and a handkerchief on his head as the other mahalas do. He is much looked to because of his knowledge of white people and their ways, and if it were not for the lines of deep sadness that fall in his face when at rest, one might forget that the woman's gear is the badge of an all but intolerable shame. At least it was so used by the Paiutes, but when you have read this full and true account of how it was first put on, you may not think it so.

Fifty years ago the valley about Tres Pinos was all one sea of moving grass and dusky, greenish sage, cropped over by deer and antelope, north as far as Togobah, and south to the Bitter Lake. Beside every considerable stream which flowed into it from the Sierras was a Paiute campoodie, and all they knew of white people was by hearsay from the tribes across the mountains. But soon enough cattlemen began to push their herds through the Sierra passes to the Paiutes' feeding-ground. The Indians saw them come, and though they were not very well pleased, they held still by the counsel of their old men; night and day they made medicine and prayed that the white men might go away.

Among the first of the cattlemen in the valley about Tres Pinos was Joe Baker, who brought a young wife, and built his house not far from the campoodie. The Indian women watched her curiously from afar because of a whisper that ran among the wattled huts. When the year was far gone, and the sun-cured grasses curled whitish brown, a doctor came riding hard from the fort at Edswick, forty miles to the south, and though they watched, they did not see him ride away. It was the third day at evening when Joe Baker came walking towards the campoodie, and his face was set and sad. He carried something rolled in a blanket, and looked anxiously at the women as he went between the huts. It was about the hour of the evening meal, and the mahalas sat about the fires watching the cooking-pots. He came at last opposite a young woman who sat nursing her child. She had a bright, pleasant face, and her little one seemed about six months old. Her husband stood near and watched them with great pride. Joe Baker knelt down in front of the mahala, and opened the roll of blankets. He showed her a day-old baby that wrinkled up its small face and cried.

"Its mother is dead," said the cattleman. The young Indian mother did not know English, but she did not need speech to know what had happened. She looked pitifully at the child, and at her husband timidly. Joe Baker went and laid his rifle and cartridge belt at the Paiute's feet. The Indian picked up the gun and fingered it; his wife smiled. She put down her own child, and lifted the little white stranger to her breast. It nozzled against her and hushed its crying; the young mother laughed.

"See how greedy it is," she said; "it is truly white." She drew up the blanket around the child and comforted it.

The cattleman called to him one of the Indians who could speak a little English.

"Tell her," he said, "that I wish her to care for the child. His name is Walter. Tell her that she is to come to my house for everything he needs, and for every month that he keeps fat and well she shall have a fat steer from my herd." So it was agreed.

As soon as Walter was old enough he came to sleep at his father's house, but the Indian woman, whom he called *Ebia*, came every day to tend him. Her son was his brother, and Walter learned to speak Paiute before he learned English. The two boys were always together, but as yet the little Indian had no name. It is not the custom among Paiutes to give names to those who have not done anything worth naming.

"But I have a name," said Walter, "and so shall he. I will call him Joe. That is my father's name, and it is a good name, too."

When Mr. Baker was away with the cattle Walter slept at the campoodie, and Joe's mother made him a buckskin shirt. At that time he was so brown with the sun and the wind that only by his eyes could you tell that he was white; he was also very happy. But as this is to be the story of how Joe came to the wearing of a woman's dress, I cannot tell you all the plays they had, how they went on their first hunting, nor what they found in the creek of Tres Pinos.

The beginning of the whole affair of Mahala Joe must be laid to the arrow-maker. The arrow-maker had a stiff knee from a wound in a long-gone battle, and for that reason he sat in the shade of his wickiup, and chipped arrow points from flakes of obsidian that young men brought him from Togobah, fitting them to shafts of reeds from the river marsh. He used to coax the boys to wade in the brown water and cut the reeds, for the dampness made his knee ache. They drove bargains with him for arrows for their own hunting, or for the sake of the stories he could tell. For an armful of reeds he would make three arrows, and for a double armful he would tell tales. These were mostly of great huntings and old wars, but when it was winter, and no snakes in the long grass to overhear, he would tell Wonder-stories. The boys would lie with their toes in the warm ashes, and the arrow-maker would begin.

"You can see," said the arrow-maker, "on the top of Waban the tall boulder looking on the valleys east and west. That is the very boundary between the Paiute country and Shoshone land. The boulder is a hundred times taller than the tallest man, and thicker through than six horses standing nose to tail; the shadow of it falls all down the slope. At mornings it falls toward the Paiute peoples, and evenings it falls on Shoshone land. Now on this side of the valley, beginning at the campoodie, you will see a row of pine trees standing all upstream one behind another. See, the long branches grow on the side toward the hill; and some may tell you it is because of the way the wind blows, but I say it is because they reach out in a hurry to get up the mountain. Now I will tell you how these things came about.

"Very long ago all the Paiutes of this valley were ruled by two brothers, a chief and a medicine man, Winnedumah and Tinnemaha. They were both very wise, and one of them never did anything without the other. They taught the tribes not to war upon each other, but to stand fast as brothers, and so they brought peace into the land. At that time there were no white people heard of, and game was plenty. The young honored old, and nothing was as it is now."

When the arrow-maker came to this point, the boys fidgeted with their toes, and made believe to steal the old man's arrows to distract his attention. They did not care to hear about the falling off of the Paiutes; they wished to have the tale. Then the arrow-maker would hurry on to the time when there arose a war between the Paiutes and the Shoshones. Then Winnedumah put on his war bonnet, and Tinnemaha made medicine. Word went around among the braves that if they stood together man to man as brothers, then they should have this war.

"And so they might," said the arrow-maker, "but at last their hearts turned to water. The tribes came together on the top of Waban. Yes; where the boulder now stands, for that is the boundary of our lands, for no brave would fight off his own ground for fear of the other's medicine. So they fought. The eagles heard the twang of the bowstring, and swung down from White Mountain. The vultures smelled the smell of battle, and came in from Shoshone land. Their wings were dark like a cloud, and underneath the arrows flew like hail. The Paiutes were the better bowmen, and they caught the Shoshone arrows where they struck in the earth and shot them back again. Then the Shoshones were ashamed, and about the time of the sun going down they called upon their medicine men, and one let fly a magic arrow,—for none other would touch him,—and it struck in the throat of Tinnemaha.

"Now when that befell," went on the arrow-maker, "the braves forgot the word that had gone before the battle, for they turned their backs to the medicine man, all but Winnedumah, his brother, and fled this way from Waban. Then stood Winnedumah by Tinnemaha, for that was the way of those two; whatever happened, one would not leave the other. There was none left to carry on the fight, and yet since he was so great a chief the Shoshones were afraid to take him, and the sun went down. In the dusk they saw a bulk, and they said, 'He is still standing;' but when it was morning light they saw only a great rock, so you see it to this day. As for the braves who ran away, they were changed to pine trees, but in their hearts they are cowards yet, therefore they stretch out their arms and strive toward the mountain. And that," said the arrow-maker, "is how the tall stones came to be on the top of Waban. But it was not in my day nor my father's." Then the boys would look up at Winnedumah, and were half afraid, and as for the tale, they quite believed it.

The arrow-maker was growing old. His knee hurt him in cold weather, and he could not make arrow points fast enough to satisfy the boys, who lost a great many in the winter season shooting at ducks in the tulares. Walter's father promised him a rifle when he was fifteen, but that was years away. There was a rock in the cañon behind Tres Pinos with a great crack in the top. When the young men rode to the hunting, they shot each an arrow at it, and if it stuck it was a promise of good luck. The boys scaled the rock by means of a grapevine ladder, and pried out the old points. This gave them an idea.

"Upon Waban where the fighting was, there must be a great many arrow points," said Walter.

"So there must be," said Joe.

"Let us go after them," said the white boy; but the other dared not, for no Paiute would go within a bowshot of Winnedumah; nevertheless, they talked the matter over.

"How near would you go?" asked Walter.

"As near as a strong man might shoot an arrow," said Joe.

"If you will go so far," said Walter, "I will go the rest of the way."

"It is a two days' journey," said the Paiute, but he did not make any other objection.

It was a warm day of spring when they set out. The cattleman was off to the river meadow, and Joe's mother was out with the other mahalas gathering taboose.

"If I were fifteen, and had my rifle, I would not be afraid of anything," said Walter.

"But in that case we would not need to go after arrow points," said the Indian boy.

They climbed all day in a bewildering waste of boulders and scrubby trees. They could see Winnedumah shining whitely on the ridge ahead, but when they had gone down into the gully with great labor, and up the other side, there it stood whitely just another ridge away.

"It is like the false water in the desert," said Walter. "It goes farther from you, and when you get to it there is no water there."

"It is magic medicine," said Indian Joe. "No good comes of going against medicine."

"If you are afraid," said Walter, "why do you not say so? You may go back if you like, and I will go on by myself."

Joe would not make any answer to that. They were hot and tired, and awed by the stillness of the hills. They kept on after that, angry and apart; sometimes they lost sight of each other among the boulders and underbrush. But it seemed that it must really have been as one or the other of them had said, for when they came out on a high mesa presently, there was no Winnedumah anywhere in sight. They would have stopped then and taken counsel but they were too angry for that, so they walked on in silence, and the day failed rapidly, as it will do in high places. They began to draw near together and to be afraid. At last the Indian boy stopped and gathered the tops of bushes together, and began to weave a shelter for the night, and when Walter saw that he made it large enough for two, he spoke to him.

"Are we lost?" he said.

"We are lost for to-night," said Joe, "but in the morning we will find ourselves."

They ate dried venison and drank from the wicker bottle, and huddled together because of the dark and the chill.

"Why do we not see the stone anymore?" asked Walter in a whisper.

"I do not know," said Joe. "I think it has gone away."

"Will he come after us?"

"I do not know. I have on my elk's tooth," said Joe, and he clasped the charm that hung about his neck. They started and shivered, hearing a stone crash far away as it rolled down the mountain-side, and the wind began to move among the pines.

"Joe," said Walter, "I am sorry I said that you were afraid."

"It is nothing," said the Paiute. "Besides, I am afraid."

"So am I," whispered the other. "Joe," he said again after a long silence, "if he comes after us, what shall we do?"

"We will stay by each other."

"Like the two brothers, whatever happens," said the white boy, "forever and ever."

"We are two brothers," said Joe.

"Will you swear it?"

"On my elk's tooth."

Then they each took the elk's tooth in his hand and made a vow that whether Winnedumah came down from his rock, or whether the Shoshones found them, come what would, they would stand together. Then they were comforted; and lay down, holding each other's hands.

"I hear some one walking," said Walter.

"It is the wind among the pines," said Joe.

A twig snapped. "What is that?" said the one boy.

"It is a fox or a coyote passing," said the other, but he knew better. They lay still, scarcely breathing, and throbbed with fear. They felt a sense of a presence approaching in the night, the whisper of a moccasin on the gravelly soil, the swish of displaced bushes springing back to place. They saw a bulk shape itself out of the dark; it came and stood over them, and they saw that it was an Indian looking larger in the gloom. He spoke to them, and whether he spoke in a strange tongue, or they were too frightened to understand, they could not tell.

"Do not kill us!" cried Walter, but the Indian boy made no sound. The man took Walter by the shoulders and lifted him up. "White," said he.

"We are brothers," said Joe; "we have sworn it."

"So," said the man, and it seemed as if he smiled.

"Until we die," said both the boys. The Indian gave a grunt.

"A white man," he said, "is—white." It did not seem as if that was what he meant to say.

"Come, I will take you to your people. They search for you about the foot of Waban. These three hours I have watched you and them." The boys clutched at each other in the dark. They were sure now who spoke to them, and between fear and fatigue and the cramp of cold they staggered and stumbled as they walked. The Indian stopped and considered them.

"I cannot carry both," he said.

"I am the older," said Joe; "I can walk." Without any more words the man picked up Walter, who trembled, and walked off down the slope. They went a long way through the scrub and under the tamarack pines. The man was naked to the waist, and had a quiver full of arrows on his shoulder. The buckthorn branches whipped and scraped against his skin, but he did not seem to mind. At last they came to a place where they could see a dull red spark across an open flat.

"That," said the Indian, "is the fire of your people. They missed you at afternoon, and have been looking for you. From my station on the hill I saw." Then he took the boy by the shoulders.

"Look you," he said, "no good comes of mixing white and brown, but now that the vow is made, see to the keeping of it." Then he stepped back from them and seemed to melt into the dark. Ahead of them the boys saw the light of the fire flare up with new fuel, and shadows, which they knew for the figures of their friends, moved between them and the flame. Swiftly as two scared rabbits they ran on toward the glow.

When Walter and Joe had told them the story at the campoodie, the Paiutes made a great deal of it, especially the arrowmaker.

"Without a doubt," he said, "it was Winnedumah who came to you, and not, as some think, a Shoshone who was spying on our land. It is a great mystery. But since you have made a vow of brothers you should keep it after the ancient use." Then he took a knife of obsidian and cut their arms, and rubbed a little of the blood of each upon the other.

"Now," he said, "you are one fellowship and one blood, and that is as it should be, for you were both nursed at one breast. See that you keep the vow."

"We will," said the boys solemnly, and they went out into the sunlight very proud of the blood upon their bared arms, holding by each other's hands.

II

When Walter was fifteen his father gave him a rifle, as he had promised, and a word of advice with it.

"Learn to shoot quickly and well," he said, "and never ride out from home without it. No one can tell what this trouble with the Indians may come to in the end."

Walter rode straight to the campoodie. He was never happy in any of his gifts until he had showed them to Joe. There was a group of older men at the camp, quartering a deer which they had brought in. One of them, called Scar-Face, looked at Walter with a leering frown.

"See," he said, "they are arming the very children with guns."

"My father promised it to me many years ago," said Walter. "It is my birthday gift."

He could not explain why, and he grew angry at the man's accusing tone, but after it he did not like showing his present to the Indians.

He called Joe, and they went over to a cave in the black rock where they had kept their boyish treasures and planned their plays since they were children. Joe thought the rifle a beauty, and turned it over admiringly in the shadow of the cave. They tried shooting at a mark, and then decided to go up Oak Creek for a shot at the gray squirrels. There they sighted a band of antelope that led them over a tongue of hills into Little Round Valley, where they found themselves at noon twelve miles from home and very hungry. They had no antelope, but four squirrels and a grouse. The two boys made a fire for cooking in a quiet place by a spring of sweet water.

"You may have my rifle to use as often as you like," said Walter, "but you must not lend it to any one in the campoodie, especially to Scar-Face. My father says he is the one who is stirring up all this trouble with the whites."

"The white men do not need any one to help them get into trouble," said Joe. "They can do that for themselves."

"It is the fault of the Indians," said Walter. "If they did not shoot the cattle, the white men would leave them alone."

"But if the white men come first to our lands with noise and trampling and scare away the game, what then will they shoot?" asked the Paiute.

Walter did not make any answer to that. He had often gone hunting with Joe and his father, and he knew what it meant to walk far, and fasting, after game made shy by the rifles of cattlemen, and at last to return empty to the campoodie where there were women and children with hungry eyes.

"Is it true," he said after a while, "that Scar-Face is stirring up all the Indians in the valley?"

"How should I know?" said Joe; "I am only a boy, and have not killed big game. I am not admitted to the counsels of the old men. What does it matter to us whether of old feuds or new? Are we not brothers sworn?"

Then, as the dinner was done, they ate each of the other's kill, for it was the custom of the Paiutes at that time that no youth should eat game of his own killing until he was fully grown. As they walked homeward the boys planned to get permission to go up on Waban for a week, after mountain sheep, before the snows began.

Mr. Baker looked grave when Walter spoke to him.

"My boy," he said, "I wish you would not plan long trips like this without first speaking to me. It is hardly safe in the present state of feeling among the Indians to let you go with them in this fashion. A whole week, too. But as you have already spoken of it, and it has probably been talked over in the campoodie, for me to refuse now would look as if I suspected something, and might bring about the thing I most fear."

"You should not be afraid for me with Joe, father, for we are brothers sworn," said Walter, and he told his father how they had mixed the blood of their arms in the arrow-maker's hut after they had come back from their first journey on Waban.

"Well," said Mr. Baker, who had not heard of this before, "I know that they set great store by these superstitious customs, but I have not much faith in the word of a Paiute when he is dealing with a white man. However, you had better go on with this hunting trip. Take Hank with you, and Joe's father, and do not be gone more than five days at the outside."

Hank was one of Mr. Baker's vaqueros, and very glad to get off for a few days' hunting on the blunt top of Waban. On the Monday following they left the Baker ranch for the mountain. As the two boys rode up the boulder-strewn slope it set them talking of the first time they had gone that way on their fruitless hunt for arrow points about the foot of Winnedumah, and of all that happened to them at that time. The valley lay below them full of purple mist, and away by the creek of Tres Pinos the brown, wattled buts of the campoodie like great wasps' nests stuck in the sage. Hank and Joe's father, with the pack horses, were ahead of them far up the trail; Joe and Walter let their own ponies lag, and the nose of one touched the flank of the other as they climbed slowly up the steep, and the boys turned their faces to each other, as if they had some vague warning that they would not ride so and talk familiarly again, as if the boiling anger of the tribes in the valley had brewed a sort of mist that rose up and gloomed the pleasant air on the slope of Waban.

"Joe," said Walter, "my father says if it came to a fight between the white settlers and the Paiutes, that you would not hold by the word we have passed."

"That is the speech of a white man," said Joe.

"But would you?" the other insisted.

"I am a Paiute," said Joe; "I will hold by my people, also by my word; I will not fight against you."

"Nor I against you, but I would not like to have my father think you had broken your word."

"Have no care," said the Indian, "I will not break it."

Mr. Baker looked anxiously after his son as he rode to the hunting on Waban; he looked anxiously up that trail every hour until the boy came again, and that, as it turned out, was at the end of three days. For the trouble among the Indians had come to something at last,—the wasps were all out of nest by the brown creeks, and with them a flight of stinging arrows. The trouble began at Cottonwood, and the hunting party on Waban the second day out saw a tall, pale column of smoke that rose up from the notch of the hill behind the settlement, and fanned out slowly into the pale blueness of the sky.

It went on evenly, neither more nor less, thick smoke from a fire of green wood steadily tended. Before noon another rose from the mouth of Oak Creek, and a third from Tunawai. They waved and beckoned to one another, calling to counsel.

"Signal fires," said Hank; "that means mischief."

And from that on he went with his rifle half cocked, and walked always so that he might keep Joe's father in full view. By night that same day there were seven smoke trees growing up in the long valley, and spreading thin, pale branches to the sky. There was no zest left in the hunt, and in the morning they owned it. Walter was worried by what he knew his father's anxiety must be. Then the party began to ride down again, and always Hank made the Indian go before. Away by the foot of Oppapago rose a black volume of smoke, thick, and lighted underneath by flames. It might be the reek of a burning ranch house. The boys were excited and afraid. They talked softly and crowded their ponies together on the trail.

"Joe," said Walter whisperingly, "if there is battle, you will have to go to it."

"Yes," said Joe.

"And you will fight; otherwise they will call you a coward, and if you run away, they will kill you."

"So I suppose," said Joe.

"Or they will make you wear a woman's dress like To-go-na-tee, the man who got up too late." This was a reminder from one of the arrow-maker's tales. "But you have promised not to fight."

"Look you," said the Indian boy; "if a white man came to kill me, I would kill him. That is right. But I will not fight you nor your father's house. That is my vow."

The white boy put out his hand, and laid it on the flank of the foremost pony. The Indian boy's fingers came behind him, and crept along the pony's back until they reached the other hand. They rode forward without talking.

Toward noon they made out horsemen riding on the trail below them. As it wound in and out around the blind gullies they saw and lost sight of them a dozen times. At last, where the fringe of the tall trees began, they came face to face. It was Mr. Baker and a party of five men; they carried rifles and had set and anxious looks.

"What will you have?" said Indian Joe's father as they drew up before him under a tamarack pine.

"My son," said the cattleman.

"Is there war?" said the Indian.

"There is war. Come, Walter."

The boys were still and scared. Slowly Hank and Walter drew their horses out of the path and joined the men. Indian Joe and his father passed forward on the trail.

"Do them no harm," said Joe Baker to those that were with him.

"Good-by, Joe," said Walter half aloud.

The other did not turn his head, but as he went they noticed that he had bared his right arm from the hunting shirt, and an inch above the elbow showed a thin, white scar. Walter had the twin of that mark under his flannels.

Mr. Baker did not mind fighting Indians; he thought it a good thing to have their troubles settled all at once in this way, but he did not want his son mixed up in it. The first thing he did when he got home was to send him off secretly by night to the fort, and from there he passed over the mountains with other of the settlers' families under strong escort, and finally went to his mother's people in the East, and was put to school. As it turned out he never came back to Tres Pinos, he does not come into this story any more.

When the first smoke rose up that showed where the fierce hate of the Paiutes had broken into flame, the Indians took their women and children away from the pleasant open slopes, and hid them in deep cañons in secret places of the rocks. There they feathered arrows, and twisted bowstrings of the sinew of deer. And because there were so many grave things done, and it was not the custom for boys to question their elders, Joe never heard how Walter had been sent away. He thought him still at the ranch with his father, and it is because of this mistake that there is any more story at all.

You may be sure that, of those two boys, Joe's was the deeper loving, for, besides having grown up together, Walter was white, therefore thinking himself, and making the other believe it, the better of the two. But for this Walter made no difference in his behavior; had Joe to eat at his table, and would have him sleep in his bed, but Joe laughed, and lay on the floor. All this was counted a kindness and a great honor in the campoodie. Walter could find out things by looking in a book, which was sheer magic, and had taught Joe to write a little, so that he could send word by means of a piece of paper, which was cleverer than the tricks Joe had taught him, of reading the signs of antelope and elk and deer. The white boy was to the Indian a little of

109

all the heroes and bright ones of the arrow-maker's tales come alive again. Therefore he quaked in his heart when he heard the rumors that ran about the camp.

The war began about Cottonwood, and ran like wildfire that licked up all the ranches in its course. Then the whites came strongly against the Paiutes at the Stone Corral, and made an end of the best of their fighting men. Then the Indians broke out in the north, and at last it came to such a pass that the very boys must do fighting, and the women make bowstrings. The cattlemen turned in to Baker's ranch as a centre, and all the northern campoodies gathered together to attack them. They had not much to hope for, only to do as much killing as possible before the winter set in with the hunger and the deep snows.

By this time Joe's father was dead, and his mother had brought the boy a quiver full of arrows and a new bowstring, and sent him down to the battle.

And Joe went hotly enough to join the men of the other village, nursing his bow with great care, remembering his father, but when he came to counsel and found where the fight must be, his heart turned again, for he remembered his friend. The braves camped by Little Round Valley, and he thought of the talk he and Walter had there; the war party went over the tongue of hills, and Joe saw Winnedumah shining whitely on Waban, and remembered his boyish errand, the mystery of the tall, strange warrior that came upon them in the night, their talk in the hut of the arrow-maker, and the vow that came afterward.

The Indians came down a ravine toward Tres Pinos, and there met a band of horses which some of their party had run in from the ranches; among them was a pinto pony which Walter had used to ride, and it came to Joe's hand when he called. Then the boy wondered if Walter might be dead, and leaned his head against the pony's mane; it turned its bead and nickered softly at his ear.

The war party stayed in the ravine until it grew dark, and Joe watched how Winnedumah swam in a mist above the hills long after the sun had gone quite down, as if in his faithfulness he would outwatch the dark; and then the boy's heart was lifted up to the great chief standing still by Tinnemaha. "I will not forget," he said. "I, too, will be faithful." Perhaps at this moment he expected a miracle to help him in his vow as it had helped Winnedumah.

In the dusk the mounted Indians rode down by the Creek of Tres Pinos. When they came by the ruined hut where his father had lived, Joe's heart grew hot again, and when he passed the arrow-maker's, he remembered his vow. Suddenly he wheeled his pony in the trail, hardly knowing what he would do. The man next to him laid an arrow across his bow and pointed it at the boy's breast.

"Coward," he whispered, but an older Indian laid his hand on the man's arm.

"Save your arrows," he said. Then the ponies swept forward in the charge, but Joe knew in an instant how it would be with him. He would be called false and a coward, killed for it, driven from the tribe, but he would not fight against his sworn brother. He would keep his vow.

A sudden rain of arrows flew from the advancing Paiutes; Joe fumbled his and dropped it on the ground. He was wondering if one of the many aimed would find his brother. Bullets answered the arrow flight. He saw the braves pitch forward, and heard the scream of wounded ponies.

He hoped he would be shot; he would not have minded that; it would be better than being called a coward. And then it occurred to him, if Walter and his father came out and found him when the fight was done, they would think that he had broken his word. The Paiutes began to seek cover, but Joe drove out wildly from them, and rode back in the friendly dark, and past the ruined campoodie, to the black rocks. There he crept into the cave which only he and Walter knew, and lay on his face and cried, for though he was an Indian he was only a boy, and he had seen his first fight. He was sick with the thought of his vow. He lay in the black rocks all the night and the day, and watched the cattlemen and the soldiers ranging all that county for the stragglers of his people, and guessed that the Paiutes had made the last stand. Then in the second night he began to work back by secret paths to the mountain camp. It never occurred to him not to go. He had the courage to meet what waited for him there, but he had not the heart to go to it in the full light of day. He came in by his mother's place, and she spat upon him, for she had heard how he had carried himself in the fight.

"No son of mine," said she.

He went by the women and children and heard their jeers. His heart was very sick. He went apart and sat down and waited what the men would say. There were few of them left about the dying fire. They had washed off their war paint, and their bows were broken. When they spoke at last, it was with mocking and sad scorn.

"We have enough of killing," said the one called Scar-Face. "Let him have a woman's dress and stay to mend the fire."

So it was done in the presence of all the camp; and because he was a boy, and because he was an Indian, he said nothing of

112

his vow, nor opened his mouth in his defense, though his heart quaked and his knees shook. He had the courage to wear the badge of being afraid all his life. They brought him a woman's dress, though they were all too sad for much laughter, and in the morning he set to bringing the wood for the fire.

Afterward there was a treaty made between the Paiutes and the settlers, and the remnant went back to the campoodie of Tres Pinos, and Joe learned how Walter had been sent out of the valley in the beginning of the war, but that did not make any difference about the woman's dress. He and Walter never met again. He continued to go about in dresses, though in time he was allowed to do a man's work, and his knowledge of English helped to restore a friendly footing with the cattlemen. The valley filled very rapidly with settlers after that, and under the slack usage of the tribe, Mahala Joe, as he came to be known, might have thrown aside his woman's gear without offense, but he had the courage to wear it to his life's end. He kept his sentence as he kept his vow, and yet it is certain that Walter never knew.